MONSTER

Little, Brown and Company

Hachette Book Group
237 Park Avenue, New York, NY 10017
Visit us at lb-kids.com

Little, Brown and Company is a division of Hachette Book Group, Inc.
The Little, Brown name and logo are trademarks of Hachette Book Group, Inc.

The publisher is not responsible for websites (or their content) that
are not owned by the publisher.

First Edition: September 2014

Library of Congress Control Number: 2014944261

ISBN 978-0-316-37737-9

10 9 8 7 6 5 4 3 2 1

RRD-C

Printed in the United States of America

MONSTER HIGH™

FREAKY FUSION

The Junior Novel

ADAPTED BY
Perdita Finn

BASED ON THE SCREENPLAY WRITTEN BY
Keith Wagner

LITTLE, BROWN AND COMPANY
New York   Boston

CHAPTER 1
A BITE-CENTENNIAL BLUNDER

A streak of lightning flashed across the sky and lit up the turrets and towers of Monster High. Thunder boomed. A storm raged. It was a typical night at the school where every kind of teen creature was accepted and welcomed. Another jagged flash illuminated a banner strung across the entrance gate. MONSTER HIGH BITE-CENTENNIAL! it proclaimed. Two hundred years of ghouls and gargoyles, specters and centaurs, vampires, mummies, zombies, and werewolves all learning together and getting along! It was time to celebrate.

But the halls of the high school were empty and quiet. A poster on the wall showed a green-faced monster happily reading a book.

The brick wall behind the poster began to shake. Bits of grit drifted toward the floor. A brick popped out. "Raaaahhhh!" screamed an unknown Creature. A cloud of dust rose into the air as a Creature burst through the wall, smashed through the poster, and rampaged down the hallway, roaring and bellowing.

A moment later, Frankie Stein poked her head through the beast-shaped hole. She had long black hair electrified with glowing white highlights, a cute scar like a beauty mark on her right cheek, and voltageous bolts on either side of her neck. She looked up the hall and down the hall, trying to figure out which way the beast had gone.

A classroom door swung open and Mr. Rotter glared at Frankie. "Frankie Stein, your assignment was to complete your scaritage report, and instead I find you running through the halls?" The teacher flipped his pencil into the air and caught it.

Frankie glanced nervously down the hallway. Where had the Creature gone? "Um…Mr. Rotter…" she began.

But before she could explain what was happening, there was an enormous crash. "Rahhhhh!" bellowed the Creature from somewhere in the school. Mr. Rotter jumped into the air and dropped his pencil.

"Your friend makes a good point." Mr. Rotter gulped, quickly stepping back inside the classroom and shutting the door.

Frankie took off in the direction of the noise— but she was running so quickly, she tripped on her platform shoes and fell to the floor.

"Graahhh!" The Creature's shadow loomed over Frankie. She screamed.

"I'll save you, Frankie!" A dashingly handsome boy with the hulking height of a zombie and a unicorn's blue horn charged down the hallway. Neighthan fell to his knees, heroically careening to the rescue like a baseball player sliding into home plate. Unfortunately, he whizzed right past Frankie and crashed into an empty classroom.

"I'm okay," he called, emerging with a wastebasket over his head. He pulled it off, threw it aside, and grabbed Frankie's hand. He pulled her into his arms and whisked her away from the beast at the very last minute. "When we get back to the others, can we skip telling them that part about the trash can?"

"My hero!" Frankie sighed, wrapping her arms around Neighthan's neck. Her bolts sparked and sizzled.

But the Creature was dangerously close. It was stomping toward them, getting closer and closer. It was about to get them when Sirena, the daughter of a mermaid and a ghost, hovered in front of it, distracting it from Frankie.

"Hey, look here!" she sang in her haunting voice. She wafted across the hallway. "Now look here!"

The Creature, confused, paused. "Rahh?"

"Now look at this!" she trilled. She flew graceful circles around the beast's head, leaving a glowing trail of ghostly haze.

"Be careful, Sirena!" Frankie warned. Neighthan was galloping away with her in his arms.

As they ran, Bonita Femur, a skeletal wraith with the wings of a giant moth, and Avia Trotter, a flying harpy with a centaur's powerful legs, hovered along beside them.

"Avia! Bonita!" Frankie was thrilled to see them both.

"Looks like you two could use a lift!" said Avia.

Both of the ghouls grabbed one of Neighthan's arms and slowly lifted the couple into the air to safety. Sirena flew toward them, and the five monsters rocketed down the hallway, each one of them a Monster High hero.

BACK TO THE BOO-GINNING

Frankie Stein stepped onto the stage in front of a projection screen. Behind her was a giant frozen image of her in Neighthan's arms with Avia, Bonita, and Sirena flying around them.

"Okay, okay, I know what you're thinking," Frankie said to the assembled students. "Who's the voltageously cute zombie-unicorn guy and could he be any more adorbs?" She paused. "That or you're wondering about the big scary monster that was chasing us. Either way, I'll bet I've sparked your attention."

Frankie snapped her fingers and a crew of ghouls and Fusions joined her on the stage. "This is a story about family," Frankie explained. "There are lots of different types of families. And they can sometimes be found in some pretty unexpected places."

Frankie snapped her fingers again and the picture on the screen changed. Avia, Bonita, Sirena, and Neighthan were all posing for a photo on the front lawn in front of Monster High. Unlike all the monsters and ghouls, they were each a combination of two different kinds of creatures. They were Fusions: freaky Fusions.

"But hey, I'm getting ahead of myself," said Frankie to the school. "Let's tell this story from the beginning." She snapped her fingers, but nothing happened.

"Ahem," coughed Frankie. "That would be the cue for the opening titles…"

She snapped one more time and her film began to roll. "It all started on the two hundredth anniversary of the opening of Monster High—the bite-centennial celebration. It was a really big deal…"

CHAPTER 3

CRUSH AT FIRST SIGHT

Students were rushing to their coffin-shaped lockers at the beginning of the day. Bite-centennial posters covered the walls, and a large banner hung from the ceiling. Frankie Stein and her ghoulfriends were admiring the decorations.

Cleo de Nile tossed her head, her gold earrings jangling. "I guess this bite-centennial celebration is a really big deal." For someone who was thousands of years old, she thought it seemed silly to fuss about anything this recent.

Clawdeen's sensitive werewolf nose twitched. "You ghouls smell that? It's like…cheap cologne."

A pair of eyeglasses floated past the ghouls. Someone invisible coughed.

"Did I say cheap?" Clawdeen hurried to correct herself. "I meant chee...eerfully applied...by our favorite invisible drama teacher. Who loves giving us A's..."

"Smooth, Clawdeen," said Cleo under her breath. "Very smooth."

Mr. Where's eyeglasses hovered near the ghouls. "Are we ready for this evening's scaritage performance, ladies?"

"Ready?" asked Frankie. "Why, we're practically bursting at the seams." She held up her arm and displayed one of her stitches.

"I know how you feel," said Mr. Where. "The whole school is howling with anticipation for the info-tainment event of the century—The *Hiss*tory of Monster High: A Bite-centennial Celebration of Exceptional Acceptance, a Mr. Where Production, Trademark Pending."

The ghouls held back their giggles.

"Do not be late for rehearsal!" Mr. Where warned as his glasses floated down the hallway.

"We won't!" called the ghouls.

As the invisible man disappeared, Clawdeen exhaled. She'd been holding her breath the whole time.

"Okay, seriously? That cologne smells worse than a zombie's gym bag. No offense, Ghoulia."

Ghoulia, one of the most stylish zombies at the school, waved her hand and groaned, grossed out as well.

As the ghouls came around the corner, they noticed a cluster of new students, books in hand. They were huddled close together and eyeing the passing students suspiciously.

"What's with the new kids?" asked Clawdeen.

Lagoona Blue, the elegant sea monster, filled them in. "They're transfer students. Fusions."

Draculaura was amazed. "You mean they're like two different monsters in one?"

"Exactly," said Lagoona. "They each have more than one scaritage." Scaritage was where monsters came from, who their grandparents were, or who'd made them or dug them up.

Cleo tightened one of the mummy wrappings on her arm. "Two different monsters? Shouldn't they have to make up their minds?"

"Cleo." Clawdeen laughed. "You can't even make up your mind when you pick an outfit for school."

"My midday outfit changes are inspiring to the other students." Cleo sniffed. "It gives them something to look forward to."

Lagoona glanced back at the new students. "I heard this isn't the first time they've changed schools. I guess being a Fusion makes it hard to fit in."

"They don't look very friendly," said Cleo.

But that's not what Frankie was thinking. She couldn't stop looking at the handsome zombie-unicorn. What a hunk! He noticed her looking at him and gave her a shy smile. Frankie, smitten, smiled back...and crashed into a bite-centennial banner in the middle of the hall and fell over.

"Oh my ghoul!" exclaimed Draculaura.

Frankie was a little dazed.

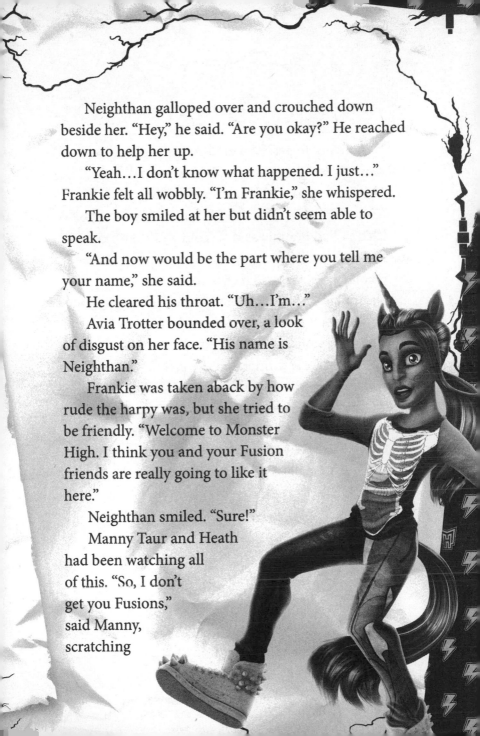

Neighthan galloped over and crouched down beside her. "Hey," he said. "Are you okay?" He reached down to help her up.

"Yeah...I don't know what happened. I just..." Frankie felt all wobbly. "I'm Frankie," she whispered.

The boy smiled at her but didn't seem able to speak.

"And now would be the part where you tell me your name," she said.

He cleared his throat. "Uh...I'm..."

Avia Trotter bounded over, a look of disgust on her face. "His name is Neighthan."

Frankie was taken aback by how rude the harpy was, but she tried to be friendly. "Welcome to Monster High. I think you and your Fusion friends are really going to like it here."

Neighthan smiled. "Sure!"

Manny Taur and Heath had been watching all of this. "So, I don't get you Fusions," said Manny, scratching the horns on his head. "Like, are you a zombie? Or are you a unicorn?"

"What's not to get?" sneered Avia. "It's like how you're a Minotaur, but you're also a slimeball."

The flames of Heath's hair sizzled. "Burn!"

"Come on, Neighthan," said Bonita. "Time to go."

Cleo pulled Frankie aside. "Told you they didn't seem very friendly."

Ghoulia groaned in agreement.

Neighthan looked down at his feet uncomfortably. "Gotta go…'bye, Frankie." He turned to follow his Fusion friends and slammed into another bite-centennial sign. He dropped to the ground but popped up immediately, embarrassed. "Heh, sign." As his friends dragged him away, he looked back over his shoulder. He couldn't take his eyes off Frankie.

Frankie watched him go. Had there ever been a cuter boy at Monster High? She didn't think so.

CHAPTER 4

SCARY SCARITAGE

Mr. Rotter was sitting at his desk twirling his pencil while Cleo gave her scaritage report in the front of the classroom. She was standing beside a massive stone slab covered in hieroglyphs. Anubis guards with doglike heads flanked the chiseled family tree. Cleo was wearing a particularly large Egyptian crown on her head as she lectured the class.

"…which brings us to the most important branch of the de Nile family tree. Next slide," she instructed the guards.

The guards pulled out hammers and chisels and began furiously chipping away at the stone slab. Stone dust flew up into the air, landing on Mr. Rotter's head. But he barely noticed. The guards stepped away and

revealed an
ancient image
of Cleo.

"So in
conclusion,"
Cleo continued,
"because my
family has more pharaohs and queens than anyone
else's, my scaritage project should win first prize."

Mr. Rotter removed his glasses, dusted them off,
and put them back on. "The scaritage report is an
assignment, not a competition."

Cleo raised a perfectly plucked eyebrow. "Just
so long as we're all in agreement that if this were a
competition, I'd win."

Mr. Rotter sighed. "Robecca Steam, your turn."

Irritated, Cleo returned to her seat while her
guards struggled to carry the enormous stone out
of the classroom. Frankie, in the front row, was
nervously holding a photo album and a rolled-up
piece of poster board.

Meanwhile, Robecca was setting up her display.
Robecca rocked her robot style with steampunk sass.
Mechanical copper legs automatically extended from

a canvas-covered portrait, creating an instant easel. Robecca cleared her throat and pulled a cord. The canvas dropped to reveal a rugged-looking man with a strong jaw and bushy mustache. He was clenching a great steam-powered mechanical arm.

"This is my father, Hexiciah Steam," explained Robecca. "He was a brilliant mechanic, a revolutionary inventor, and a teacher here at Monster High."

Mr. Rotter looked smug. "I was well acquainted with Professor Steam. I was his favorite student. And who could blame him?" He flipped his pencil into the air, fumbled, and dropped it.

Robecca continued. "My father had a workshop down in the catacombs where they say he invented something new every single day." She smiled. "And one day, he invented *me*!"

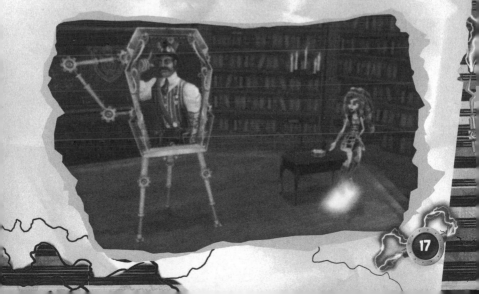

Mr. Rotter pointed at himself. "Favorite student. Right here." He tried to flip his pencil and, again, he dropped it.

Robecca held up an elaborate box constructed of hexagonal metal panels. "This belonged to my father." She set it down on a small shelf that extended from the easel. As she did so, a series of magnifying lenses emerged from it, giving the class a much closer look at its detail.

The class was studying it with a great deal of curiosity. What was it? What did it do? How was it related to Robecca's scaritage?

But Robecca didn't have any answers. "I don't really know what it is," she told the class. "Father went missing more than one hundred years ago, so I've kept this to remember him by. Every time I look at it, it reminds me how grateful I am that Hexiciah discovered the secret to creating life…to creating me."

Everyone clapped supportively. Mr. Rotter beamed at her. "Very good, Robecca. And now…Frankie Stein."

Frankie stared at Mr. Rotter, frozen with fright. Finally, she stood up, clutching her photo album. She was visibly shaking.

She tried to smile. She waved at the class. "Um…
hi…how's everybody doing?"

"I'm good!" shouted Heath in response.

"Quiet, you," snapped Mr. Rotter. He turned to
Frankie. "You're stalling."

"Right." Frankie took a big breath. "My scaritage.
So…my grandfather was
Victor Frankenstein
and he built my
dad, and that's all I
know. Thank you."

She was
headed back to
her seat when Mr.
Rotter stopped her.
"That's it?"

"I th-think Grandpa went to
Monster High," she stuttered, close to tears. "Oh, and
I have these." She unrolled a set of life-size blueprints.
"These are for making me," she explained.

"And the photo album?" questioned Mr. Rotter.

Frankie held it up. There was nothing inside it
but ripped-out pages. "That's all I've got. Thank you."

Mr. Rotter shook his head. "Frankie Stein, I

am most disappointed with this report. You are completely unprepared."

"But my mom and dad won't tell me about my—"

But Mr. Rotter wasn't listening. "When I was a student here at Monster High, I was always prepared. It's like Professor Steam always used to say, *If you're always prepared…*"

"*You'll never be scared,*" completed the class, who'd heard this about a hundred times before from Mr. Rotter.

"Correct," said Mr. Rotter. "Frankie Stein, you are to redo this assignment and present it again first thing tomorrow. Abbey Bominable, you have the floor."

The icy-cool daughter of a yeti strode to the front of the class in her shaggy fur boots. Following along behind her was a pair of yaks pulling a frozen ice block. Abbey tossed her mane of long white hair and began speaking in her thick Russian accent. "Family history starts with Ice Age. Fasten seat belts. This could take while."

Frankie sank down in her seat, more embarrassed than ever. What was she going to do about her project when her scaritage was such a family secret?

CHAPTER 5

SNACK ATTACK

Frankie sat with her friends in the Creepateria, but she didn't feel like eating. She couldn't stop thinking about her project. The other girls were chatting away.

"Could somebody pass the dead sea salt?" asked Clawdeen. Beside her lunch tray was an open sketchbook filled with fashion ideas.

"I've got it!" said Draculaura, reaching for the salt at the same moment that Robecca also extended her hand.

"Sorry about that," Robecca apologized.

"After you," said Draculaura.

They both reached for the salt, knocked it over, and apologized to each other.

"Oh, for dying out loud!" Clawdeen grabbed it herself.

Lagoona noticed that Frankie was almost as blue as she was. "Don't fret, love. A bad grade on your project isn't the end of the world."

"No, it's not that, Lagoona." Frankie sighed. "It's just…you ghouls all seem to know so much about your scaritage. But I don't know anything about mine."

Ghoulia was examining Robecca's mysterious mechanical box. Ghoulia could only speak in moans and groans, but she was still the cleverest student at Monster High.

"Can you not speak to your father about your family?" suggested Jinafire. She was part dragon and all spice.

Frankie shook her head. "My parents won't talk about my grandfather. And any time I ask, my dad just gets into one of his moods and is all, you know…" She held up her arms and began making guttural noises like the classic stereotype of a Frankenstein monster.

Ghoulia was poking at the box. She held it up to her ear and listened to it.

Lagoona took a sip of her soup. "Ooh. Too cold."

"Allow me." Jinafire blew a blast of dragon breath into the bowl. Flames erupted.

"Much better," said Lagoona sarcastically.

Suddenly Frankie's face lit up. Neighthan and the Fusions were walking by with their trays. "Hey, guys," she called. "Want to join us?"

Neighthan began walking toward the table. "That would be—"

"Unnecessary," sneered Avia Trotter, stopping him. "We've already got a table, thanks."

Neighthan looked back over his shoulder at Frankie, clearly disappointed.

Cleo was not impressed. "Rude much? No wonder they got kicked out of eight different schools."

Robecca was lost in thought. She was trying to see if there was some way she could help Frankie with her project. After all, Frankie's grandfather had been a student of her father's. "You know, I wish there were some way we could find my father's workshop in the catacombs. He used to keep a journal about everything. I bet he wrote about your grandfather."

"Do you remember where it is?" asked Draculaura.

Robecca closed her eyes and concentrated. Her gears sped up. She whirred and clanked and steamed a little. She opened her eyes. "If I really fire on all cylinders, I think I might be able to find it."

"Well, what are we waiting for?" asked Venus McFlytrap. Her excitement caused the salad in front of her to sprout vines that climbed off her tray and crept onto Clawdeen's sketchbook.

"Venus, you're doing it again. You know I don't do salad." Clawdeen, a total carnivore, swiped the vine and cut it off. She studied her sketchbook, displeased. She could not solve this one style problem. "I just can't figure out his new look. Maybe a little trip to the catacombs will help me find some inspiration."

Toralei, the gossip-loving werecat, overheard her and came over to the table. "What's this I hear about a mystery trip to the catacombs? I'm so there," she purred. She sidled in next to Cleo. "Scooch."

"Um, hello," said Cleo, pushing Toralei away. "This is *my* space. And why would you want to come with us to the catacombs, Toralei?"

"I'm a curious kitty," she said. "Now let's go find that…whatever it is we're finding." She brushed up against Cleo just like a cat as all the ghouls stood up. Frankie lingered for a moment before leaving the Creepateria. The Fusions were sitting alone at a table in the corner.

Clawdeen took Frankie by the arm. "All right, loverghoul, let's go."

Across the room, Neighthan watched Frankie leave with her friends. "I don't see why we couldn't sit with them. Those ghouls seemed nice."

Bonita was nervously chewing on the edge of her sleeve.

"Don't be dense, Neighthan," said Avia. "Regular monsters don't want anything to do with us Fusions. You know how it works. We change schools, get pushed around for a few weeks, then it's off to find another school. This place will be no different."

But Neighthan didn't agree with her. "Come on, Avia, Monster High is supposed to be different than those other schools. They say everyone is welcome here. Even if they have a freaky flaw."

Bonita pulled her sleeve out of her mouth. "Yeah, *flaw*...not *flaws*. They don't understand what it's like to have two. Right, Sirena? Sirena?"

But Sirena wasn't listening. She was piling up her mashed potatoes like wet sand to make a little castle. "Huh? Oh. Yes. I agree with all of you." She didn't even look up.

Avia Trotter shook her head. "You got distracted again."

"No, I just..." Sirena noticed the potatoes on Avia's plate. "Hey, are you going to finish those?"

Avia sighed and pushed her tray across the table. Sirena happily began adding turrets to her potato castle. Sometimes even Avia got tired of Sirena's freaky flaws.

6

CRYPT TRIP

The ghouls wound their way through the crumbling tombstones on the front lawn toward the entrance to the catacombs. They came to an old crypt with cellar-style doors that opened right into the ground. Stone gargoyles decorated the entranceway. Robecca pulled on one of the ugly statue's tongues and immediately, the doors of the crypt opened. An old wrought-iron elevator rose up in front of them.

"After you," said Robecca to Draculaura.

"No, please, you first," said Draculaura politely.

"Thank you," they said simultaneously. They entered the elevator together, squeezed through, got stuck…and fell on top of each other. The other ghouls followed and the gate clanged shut. Down, down the elevator went to the catacombs.

Inside, Toralei was pushing against Cleo for more space. "Move over," said Cleo, irritated.

"I like this spot," Toralei purred, jostling Cleo again.

The elevator banged to a stop and the doors opened in front of a spiral staircase. Down, down they climbed farther under the school. At last they emerged before a dark tunnel. Robecca stopped, shut her eyes, and whirred. Which direction was her father's laboratory?

Venus, bursting with excitement, released a haze of pollen into the air.

"Achoo!" sneezed Clawdeen. "Easy with the pollen, Venus. Werewolves are allergic."

Robecca opened her eyes and pointed. "That way."

The ghouls followed her through the blackness of the catacombs. The mournful notes of a distant organ echoed through the winding passageway. Ghoulia held Hexiciah's box to her ear, but the music was coming from Operetta the phantom practicing in an underground chamber.

She looked up as the ghouls entered. "Enjoying a little midday stroll through the catacombs?" she asked.

"Hey, Operetta," called out Draculaura, relieved. "I forgot how totes creepy it is down here."

"Aw, don't worry," drawled the phantom. "I've been all over these catacombs and there's nothing to be scared of."

Robecca shut her eyes again and pointed to a tunnel on the other side of the chamber.

Operetta looked surprised. "Shoot, y'all didn't say you were going into the *uncharted* catacombs. Nobody's been down that way for centuries. Goooooood luck." She picked up her hands and began playing a dirge fit for a funeral.

"Okay," said Draculaura nervously. "Good talk…" She followed the others into the pitch darkness.

"Can anybody see anything?" asked Venus.

"I've got this," said Jinafire. She released a blast of fire that lit up the torches lining the walls of the tunnel. The good news was that they could see; the bad news was that a long trench of water blocked their way.

"No, mate, I've got this!" said Lagoona. She dove beneath the water, and a moment later the ghouls could hear it gushing out of an invisible drain. When it was all gone, there was Lagoona holding a giant plug. The ghouls climbed down a staircase toward her and continued exploring the catacombs.

They wound this way and that, all the time going farther and farther underground.

Finally, the tunnel came to a dead end—in front of a huge circular door with the face of a grandfather clock. From behind it, the ghouls could hear the sound of ticking. *Tick, tick, tick.*

"This is it!" announced Robecca. "Ghouls, I give you the workshop of Hexiciah Steam!"

She spun a wheel on the door, unlocking it. It clanked open, but there was no workshop—only an empty chasm.

Draculaura gulped. She threw one of the torches into the hole. Down, down it fell, growing smaller and smaller. They waited to hear it land. But it didn't. It seemed to fall forever. "I didn't expect it to be so... so...bottomless pitty."

The door in front of the ghouls slammed shut for no apparent reason.

"I don't understand," said Robecca, confused. "The workshop should be right here." She spun the wheel on the door again. It clanked open, but instead of the chasm, there was a giant dragon sitting atop a mound of golden treasure!

"Ahhh!" screamed the ghouls.

The dragon opened his mouth to breathe fire, but they managed to slam the door shut in the nick of time.

"All those in favor of not opening the scary clock door again, say *eyeball*," said Clawdeen.

Ghoulia was examining the mysterious box again.

She twisted one of the hexagonal plates and something inside of it clicked. She could hear something ticking. *Tick, tick, tick.* Just like with the door.

Carefully, Ghoulia placed the box on the ground. As she stepped away, panels unfolded, gears began to turn, and the entire device miraculously transformed into a miniature likeness of a workshop.

Draculaura studied it, amazed. "Okay, question. Was your father really, really tiny?"

Robecca shook her head. "I don't get it. It's just a model."

Ghoulia bent down to study the workshop. On its floor were two arrows, each pointing in a different direction, like the hands of a clock. There was a button at their center, and Ghoulia pushed it. Immediately, the device began

cranking and wheezing. The arrows slowly edged
forward and stopped at the time 12:55.

Ghoulia groaned in understanding.

"It's about time?" translated Venus.

"She's right," said Cleo, fed up. "It's about time we
got out of here."

Ghoulia moaned. *No, no*, she seemed to be saying.
She went over to the door and began spinning the
wheel. *Tick, tick, tick*. She turned the wheel and
stopped when the hands of the clock on the door said
12:55. *Click!* The door opened again, but this time
behind them was the workshop.

"It's about *time!*" exclaimed Robecca delightedly.
"A security lock based on a clock system. That is so my
dad."

Ghoulia scooped up the model and folded it back
into the box.

One by one, the ghouls entered the long-lost
workshop. Would they find Hexiciah's journals?
Would there be any information about Victor
Frankenstein? Frankie hoped so—it was the only hope
she had.

CHAPTER 7

GONE, GHOUL, GONE

The workshop was a cobweb-covered mess. Gears, springs, bottles, and all kinds of mechanical parts littered the floor. Chains hung from the beams and catwalks. Old copper valves and pipes lined the walls. There were piles of torn blueprints and sketches on the scattered workbenches. On one were steam boots just like the jet-powered ones Robecca wore, only bigger and covered in dust. Everything was covered in dust. At the far end of the circular room was a rusted recharge chamber.

In the very center of the room was a huge platform. Held in place by magnets was a huge crystal lens lined with copper. It too was covered in rust and dust and spiderwebs.

As the ghouls entered the chamber, a cuckoo clock began to strike. A cuckoo bird emerged through a film of cobwebs, coughing; let out a single strained "cuckoo"; and returned inside the clock.

Robecca took everything in. It had been a long time since she'd been here. "Okay, everybody, spread out and look for that journal," she ordered her friends. "But remember, don't touch anything." She stared at Toralei, who had enough curiosity for ten ghouls.

"Why's everybody looking at me?" she hissed.

No one said a word.

"Okay, don't touch anything, got it!" she conceded.

The ghouls spread out to investigate. Robecca searched through an enormous stack of books. Cleo walked over to the floating lens in the middle of the room. It bobbed up and down between the two magnets. Beside the lens was a massive control panel. It was covered in tubes and switches and a tangle of wires. Cleo peered to study the lens in awe. "Oh… my…Ra!"

She looked closer and closer. What did she see? "Why didn't anybody tell me my headband was crooked?" She smoothed her hair back into place.

Toralei popped up behind the lens, her striped cat face magnified. "Whatcha doin'?" she asked.

Cleo jumped back in surprise. "Toralei!"

Toralei gave the lens a little shove. It swung forward then snapped back into place between the magnets. "Me-ow," she yowled.

Robecca gasped. "Ghouls! I found the journal!"

Frankie rushed over. "Does it say anything about my grandfather?"

Robecca flipped through the pages, scanning them. She smiled at Frankie. "*October Fifth, 1814. Victor Frankenstein is one of the brightest and most promising students I have ever had the pleasure to educate,*" she read out loud.

"That's him!" exclaimed Frankie. "You found my grandfather! What else does it say?"

Robecca skimmed through the journal. "Let's see. *Superior intellect. Hungry for knowledge… Unfortunately, there's another side to Victor. A dangerous inner personality that recklessly disregards the spectacular mysteries of life in pursuit of his scientific ambitions. I fear this may be young Victor's undoing…*"

Frankie was stunned. "Wow. I wonder if that's why my parents don't talk about him."

Cleo was still adjusting her hair in the lens when it started to spin on its side like a coin. "Hey!" she exclaimed. "I wasn't done with that." She stepped back as it spun faster and faster.

A swirling blue vortex began to emerge from the lens.

"That's different," said Cleo, a little alarmed.

Everyone turned to stare. Toralei was standing by the control panel. She looked guilty. "Okay," she admitted. "Now I get why you all looked at me when you said don't touch anything."

"Toralei!" screamed everyone.

The blue vortex was pulling everyone in the room toward it. Toralei lifted off the ground and grabbed one of the chains hanging from the catwalk. The catwalk itself began to tumble toward the vortex. The ghouls screamed. They were going to be sucked right into it! The journal fell out of Robecca's hands. One by one, each of the ghouls was swallowed  into the lens and disappeared. The blue light flickered. The machine died down. The ghouls were gone.

CHAPTER 8

FREAKY FLASHBACK!

The ghouls woke up sprawled across the floor of the workshop. Everything was exactly the same, except the dust and cobwebs were gone. The pipes shone, the gears were polished, and even the cuckoo clock looked shiny and new. The bird emerged and let out one crystal clear "Cuckoo!"

The ghouls sat up, dazed and in pain.

"Somebody wanna guess what just happened?" asked Lagoona, rubbing her head.

"I'll tell you what happened," said Cleo. "Toralei touched something."

Toralei stretched. "Look, we can argue all day about who touched what. The important thing is, I'm fine."

Draculaura blinked. "Something's different. Does this workshop look…cleaner to you ghouls?"

Venus agreed. "Draculaura's right. Something *is* different."

"Isn't it obvious?" Toralei shrugged. "Robecca's dad invented some kind of cleaner-upper machine. You ghouls should thank me for sprucing up this dump."

"Whatever that was," Jinafire said thoughtfully, "I feel it would be wise for us to leave before something else happens."

"Jinafire's right," agreed Clawdeen. "We should get back up to school or we're gonna miss Mr. Where's rehearsal."

The ghouls dusted themselves off and headed out the door, back through the catacombs. Frankie was the last to leave. Something was bothering her, but she couldn't figure out what exactly. She took a last look around the workshop. It was just so…clean. But at least she had what she needed for her project.

After a journey back through the tunnels, they emerged from the crypt into daylight. Ghoulia's eyes were the first to adjust to the brightness—and she couldn't believe what she was seeing. She groaned, she pointed, she moaned.

All the ghouls turned to look.

Only the main building of Monster High stood in front of them. The rest was still under construction with scaffolding around the bare beams of the towers. A banner strung across the front door read WELCOME TO MONSTER HIGH—1814.

A carriage drawn by a skeleton horse stopped by the front steps. Ghouls in long, flouncy skirts held parasols over their heads. A skeleton janitor was pumping water into a bucket. He stopped to take a drink, and the water poured right through him to the ground. Then he went back to pumping.

The ghouls couldn't believe what they were seeing.

Draculaura was the first to find her voice. "1814? So that means Hexiciah Steam built…"

"A time teleporter," completed Robecca, awed.

This was better than a journal, Frankie realized. "If this is 1814, then that means I can go meet my grandfather!"

Ghoulia shook her head vehemently.

"I agree," said Jinafire. "We cannot risk interactions with past events. Our presence here could change the entire course of monster history."

Frankie was disappointed. "I guess you're right."

But something else was worrying Robecca. "Ghoulia, how long until we can open the workshop door again?"

Ghoulia opened Hexiciah's box, pressed a button, and waited. After a minute, she groaned the answer.

"Then it's settled," said Clawdeen. "We wait one hour for the workshop door to reopen, and then we go back to…" Her voice trailed off. She glanced across the lawn. "Where's Toralei?"

The ghouls panicked. The werecat was nowhere in sight.

At last Cleo spotted her heading up the front doors into the school. "That kitty really rankles my bandages."

"We've got to find her before she causes any more trouble," said Frankie.

"Oh, this is so bad." Draculaura sighed.

"Don't worry," Lagoona said reassuringly. "We'll catch Toralei."

"Not that," cried Draculaura in a sheer panic. She

held up her phone. "There's no iCoffin reception in 1814!"

But there were bigger differences than that.

In the main hallway, students were staring at the ghouls, looking them up and down.

"Why's everyone staring at us?" asked Draculaura.

"It's 1814," Clawdeen pointed out. "They've never seen styles like ours before."

It was true. If some of the fashions were the same—the high boots, the corsets, the gloves, the pleats, and the lace—the lengths of the skirts were distinctly different. None of the ghouls in 1814 were showing their knees…or even their ankles.

One skeleton came over to Cleo and touched the fabric of her sleeve. Cleo slapped her bony hand. "It's a Ghost-ier original and it's magnificent. Move along."

"The sooner we find Toralei and get back to our own time, the better," said Lagoona.

"We should split up," suggested Frankie. "We'll find her faster that way. Let's meet up back at the workshop door."

"And remember," said Jinafire as they divided into two groups going in opposite directions, "try not to talk to *anybody*."

9

NORMIE KNOW-HOW

Frankie and Ghoulia walked along the hallway, peeking into classrooms. They were filled with busy students—but there was no sign of Toralci. The whistle of a steam train from a lab startled Frankie and Ghoulia, who rushed to see what was going on. The classroom was arranged like a theater and the seats were filled with chattering monsters. The room was dark, lit only by candles, and the ghouls were able to sneak in without anyone noticing.

A trapdoor hissed, emitted a plume of steam, and opened. Out of it stepped a tall, broad man with a steam-powered mechanical arm.

"That's Hexiciah Steam, Robecca's dad," Frankie whispered to Ghoulia.

"All right, class. Settle, settle!" he announced.

A stumpy boy, out of breath and green-hued, hurried past Frankie and Ghoulia, bumping into them.

"Sorry I'm late, Professor S-Steam!" he stuttered. "Again."

"Oh. My. Ghoul!" exclaimed Frankie, realizing who it was.

"Mr. Rotter!" reprimanded Professor Steam. Clearly the boy was not one of his favorite students. "Just take your seat. I trust you're prepared to deliver your scaritage report?"

The teenage Mr. Rotter hemmed and hawed. "I... um...no, sir."

The professor sighed. "A little preparation would go a long way toward succeeding in my class, Mr. Rotter. You see, if you're always prepared..."

"You'll never be scared!" completed Frankie.

Hexiciah grinned at her, amused. "Yes, very good. I like that."

Frankie and Ghoulia slipped into seats in the back of the classroom. Ghoulia whispered a groan to Frankie.

"I know," Frankie answered. "I can't believe Robecca is missing this. I wish I could text her." She sighed, thinking of her useless iCoffin. How did these students manage without them?

At the front of the room, Professor Steam was lecturing the class. "Now then, since Mr. Rotter is not prepared…"

As if on cue, Rotter flipped his pencil into the air and dropped it.

Hexiciah Steam glared at him, shaking his head. "Would somebody *else* care to share something about their scaritage?"

"I've got this," announced a boy in the front row. He was a thin kid with straight black hair—a normie. He was wearing a lab coat and his feet were propped up on his desk as if this class was the easiest thing he did all day long. Frankie and Ghoulia stared at him. There was something familiar about him, but what was it?

"All right then, Sparky." Hexiciah Steam sighed. "You're next."

The boy rose out of his seat and sauntered to the front of the classroom.

"Check out mad scientist boy," Frankie whispered to Ghoulia.

Sparky had wheeled in a medical gurney. Covered in a white sheet were two body-size mounds.

"Class, Professor Steam. I do not have a scaritage. For, you see, I am an orphan. So…because I don't have a family…*I made one!*" He gave the lever on the gurney a hard crank and it tilted forward. The sheet rolled down, revealing two robotic monsters. They were crude—made out of bits of discarded junk, burlap, and a few strange humanlike parts.

The Creatures extended their hands and began moaning and growling.

There were gasps from the students.

"Yes!" proclaimed Sparky. "I have created *life*! Feast your eyes upon Genealogi-bots 3.5 and 3.7. Don't ask about 3.6. He turned out to be a few electrons short of a carbon molecule, if you know what I mean."

One of the monster's hands dangled from his wrist and fell off, with a flat *thud*, to the floor. Flustered, Sparky picked it up and tried to wedge it back onto the monster's arm. "Not to worry." He smiled through gritted teeth. "Just a little setback."

As he fidgeted with the monster, it tipped to its side, knocking into the other creature—whose head wobbled and fell off.

"Maybe the normie student exchange program wasn't such a good idea," muttered a student in the back of the classroom.

"Think we should send him back?" asked a ghoul.

First one student laughed and then another, until the whole class was roaring.

Sparky shook the monster's unattached hand at them, like he was scolding them. "Stop laughing at me! I can get it right; I know it. I'm just...I'm just missing something. Some part. Some ingredient!"

Hexiciah had been watching all of this, deep in thought. He silenced the class with a wave of his hand. He turned to Sparky. "You're right. You are missing something. You tried to create life using this." He pointed at Sparky's head. "But you left out this." He poked the center of Sparky's chest—right where his heart would be.

Sparky's brow furrowed, trying to figure out what his teacher was saying. "You mean guts and organs and stuff? No, I used plenty of those. Look..." He began to rummage through the monsters, but Hexiciah stopped him.

"No!" bellowed the teacher passionately. "What I'm talking about isn't a physical part, lad. Not some tangible ingredient. Creating life requires something more…Something…of one's self…a spark."

Sparky was baffled. "You lost me."

Hexiciah addressed the whole class. "There are two sides to every single one of us. There's this physical nonsense of skin and bones—and in some cases copper and steel…" He grinned as he released a slow whistle of steam from his mechanical arm. "But there's also something deep down that we can't see or touch. Maybe it's emotion, maybe it's love, I don't really know."

Sparky wasn't buying any of this. He could barely disguise his impatience.

Hexiciah shook his head. "But what I do know is that you cannot simply use the brute force of science to cater to your every whim. If you're not careful, the consequences could be catastrophic."

In the back row, Frankie looked down at her own hand, carefully sewn to her wrist. This had all felt very personal to her. "But it *is* possible," she whispered to Ghoulia. "Somebody made me…"

Sparky thought his teacher was ridiculous. "*Sparks! Love!*" he said mockingly. "That doesn't make

any sense. I will figure out how to create life. I will make it work. And then, I will be the one laughing at all of you!"

The monster hand that Sparky had been holding suddenly came to life and wrapped itself around his face. "Get it off! Get it off!" the boy screamed. He flailed, trying to whip it off. Unable to see, he ran into the wall and knocked himself backward to the ground. The hand jumped off his face and scrambled out the door. The class exploded with more laughter.

All except for Frankie. She felt sorry for Sparky for some reason she couldn't explain.

Hexiciah offered the boy his mechanical hand to help him get up, but Sparky wouldn't take it. He got up on his own.

"Why don't we continue this discussion after class?" Hexiciah suggested kindly. "Come find me in my workshop. I'll be in my Recharge Chamber."

"I will create life!" Sparky yelled defiantly. "I'll show all of you!" He stormed out of the classroom, ignoring his teacher's offer.

Tears welled up in Frankie's eyes. "Poor Sparky." She slipped out of her seat and followed him out of the classroom.

Throughout all of this, Rotter had been scribbling in his notebook. He raised his hand. "Professor Steam? Will any of that be on the final exam? Trying to, you know, be prepared." He flipped his pencil into the air and it bonked him on the top of his head.

Hexiciah sighed. "Mr. Rotter, you are far and away my least favorite student."

SPARKS FLY

At the very top of the partially constructed tower of the high school, Sparky had built himself a laboratory. Broken test tubes and rusted coils littered the floor of the scaffolding. Sparky himself was standing on an old operating table trying to fix a bent lightning rod mounted on the makeshift roof. He swung a wrench at it, missed, and swung again. He was clearly upset and talking to himself.

"Sign up for the Normie Exchange Program, Sparky! It'll be a great way to expand your horizons, Sparky! I'm sick of expanding my horizons. I like them just fine the way they are. I like medium-size horizons."

Someone was climbing up the stairs toward him.

He could hear footsteps.

"Sparky? Are you okay?" It was Frankie.

Sparky gave her a look of utter contempt and swung his wrench again. "What do you want? Here to make fun of me too?"

"No," Frankie said softly. "I just…I don't know, wanted to tell you that I understand how you feel."

"What?" sneered Sparky. "You're an orphan too?"

"No. But I understand what it's like to not know about your scaritage. It makes you feel lost. And sad. But you're lucky you get to go to a school like Monster High—where everybody can be like your family."

Sparky turned on her, his eyes blazing with fury. "Family? Pah! Those nitwits aren't fit to be in my family. Which is why I'm going to create one. If I can just figure out how…" He strained and grunted trying to reach the lightning rod.

"Here," offered Frankie. She popped off her hand and sent it crawling up the operating table. It grabbed a cable and pulled itself toward the lightning rod. It tightened the bolts and straightened it.

Sparky was stunned. "How…how can you do that?"

"Well, because I was created," explained Frankie. "And my father was too. In a lab."

Her hand waved down at them in agreement.

"So it *is* possible!" exclaimed Sparky. "I knew it! But how?"

Frankie shrugged. "I don't know. I guess my grandfather somehow figured out that missing spark Professor Steam was talking about."

Sparky hopped off the table and grabbed Frankie by the shoulders, behaving exactly like a mad scientist. "You have to tell me how it's done! Who is your grandfather? What is the secret? *What am I missing?*"

Frankie was frightened. She'd made a big mistake. She saw that now. They weren't even supposed to talk to anybody in the past. "I shouldn't have said anything. I'm sorry. I have to go!" She broke away and hurried down the tower stairs, her detached hand scrambling after her.

Sparky, his thoughts racing, watched her go.

Frankie ran across the lawn, dodging tombstones. She fixed her hand back to her wrist. The other ghouls were already waiting at the entrance to the crypt. Lagoona and Jinafire were on either side of Toralei, each holding one of her arms.

"Hey, Frankie, look who we found," said Jinafire.

Toralei struggled to break free. "You know, one day we are gonna look back on this and laugh."

The ghouls got in the elevator and the gate closed behind them.

"You really did it this time, mate," said Lagoona. "Your little stunt nearly caused us a lot of trouble."

"Since when has a little curiosity caused *any* trouble?" she asked innocently.

Everyone glared at her.

"Oh right." Toralei shrugged. "The whole *accidentally sending us back in time* thing. My bad."

From the tower, Sparky had been watching Frankie meet up with her friends and get in the elevator. He couldn't stop thinking about what she had said. Who had made her? How? He had to find out!

When they reached Hexiciah's workshop, the ghouls stepped aside to let Ghoulia make some final adjustments to the time portal's controls. Robecca had discovered that Hexiciah was asleep, standing upright, in his Recharge Chamber.

Her face was full of love for her talented father. "He built this Recharge Chamber. Said it would give him a boost of energy when he was inventing things." Robecca reached out and lightly touched his chest. "I wish we could have had more time."

The lens was beginning to spin. The time portal was opening.

"That's our ride!" said Cleo. "You ghouls coming?"

"Just try and stop me!" Draculaura was desperate

to get back. "If I don't get my eyes on a gossip blog soon, I'm gonna go batty."

Robecca wrote a note on a scrap piece of paper. *Hi, Dad. I miss you. Love, your daughter.* She attached it to his Recharge Chamber with a magnet.

Draculaura was about to enter the portal when she stepped aside for Robecca. "After you."

"No, please, you first," said Robecca. They were having their usual war of politeness.

"I insist." Draculaura didn't budge.

Clawdeen sighed. "Are we really going to do this again?"

"Wait!" Sparky barged into the workshop, breathing hard and covered in cobwebs. "You can't leave yet! You have to show me how to create life!"

Cleo turned to Frankie. "Friend of yours?"

"You shouldn't be here!" exclaimed Frankie.

"You need to help me!" Sparky's eyes were wild. "I need to create my family."

Ghoulia groaned. This was exactly what shouldn't have happened.

"Ghoulia's right," Lagoona urged. "We have to go!"

Frankie was about to cry. "I have to go back where I belong."

Sparky leaped forward. "Take me with you!" Sparky crashed into a bookshelf, setting off a chain reaction. The bookshelves crashed into one another like dominoes. The last bookshelf hit a table, catapulting it forward and hurling a loose screwdriver across the room. It landed on the control panel to the time portal. The machine sparked. The blue vortex flickered. The lens wobbled between the magnets.

In the corner, Hexiciah snored away, oblivious to the chaos.

"Whoops!" said Sparky.

Ghoulia dove into the portal, ordering the others to follow. Lagoona grabbed Jinafire and pulled her into the vortex. Cleo took hold of Toralei's shoulders and they tumbled in together. "In you go, calico!"

Draculaura and Robecca held hands and jumped, as did Clawdeen and Venus.

Frankie wavered.

"So that's it?" said Sparky. "You're just going to leave without helping me?"

Frankie shook her head. "I'm going to look you up when I get home, Sparky. I've got a feeling you're going to create something wonderful here at Monster High." She leaped into the portal and disappeared.

But that wasn't good enough for Sparky. He charged at the portal and dove in at the last possible moment. The lens stopped spinning. The portal closed. Everything was quiet in the workshop.

A timer dinged and the door to the Recharge Chamber opened. Hexiciah Steam stretched and yawned. "Most refreshing. Now then, what say we take another crack at that Steamatronic Temporal Teleport…"

Hexiciah looked at his invention, stunned. It was destroyed. The control panel emitted a last dying hiss.

"Or I could work on something else." Hexiciah sighed.

That's when he saw Robecca's note. He read it, confused. "*Love, your daughter*? Hmmm, now there's a challenge…a daughter."

He picked up a pencil and began sketching some blueprints for a robot girl. What should she look like? Should he give her rocket boots? But of course!

FUSED! Can eight ghouls in four bodies ever get along?

Frankie Stein's the star of the Monster High bite-centennial celebration!

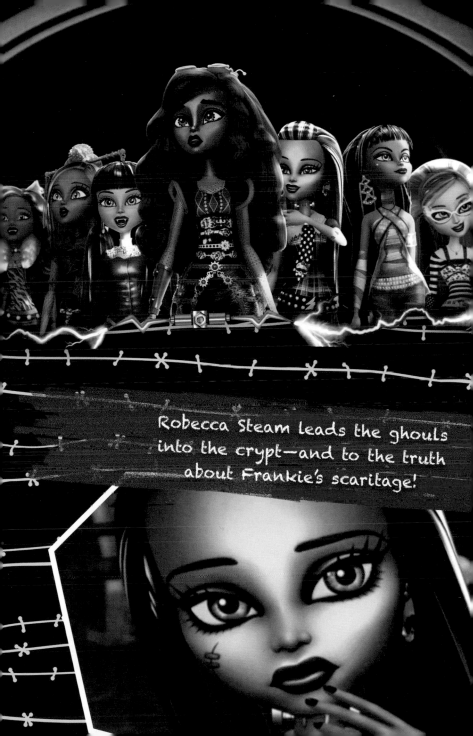

Robecca Steam leads the ghouls into the crypt—and to the truth about Frankie's scaritage!

Sparks fly when this mad scientist hops a ride to the future.

Fusions to the rescue!

Cleolei gets a lesson in chill from the hottest zombie-unicorn at Monster High

Ghoulia Yelps's mission? Fix the teleporter—before it's too late.

Frankie's special spark saves the day!

Enter the blue vortex between the worlds. . . .

The ghouls tumbled through the swirling vortex, clinging to one another. Wild flashes of energy shot through them like x-rays. At last they saw a pinprick of light from the workshop rising toward them.

"Hang on!" called Clawdeen as they crashed to a landing.

Sparky saw the ghouls in a pile in front of him. But just as he was about to burst out of the vortex, the portal closed. He was stuck between the worlds. Lost in time!

"Noooooooo!" he shouted, whirling around and around in nothingness.

In the workshop, Frankie and Ghoulia sat up, dazed from the journey.

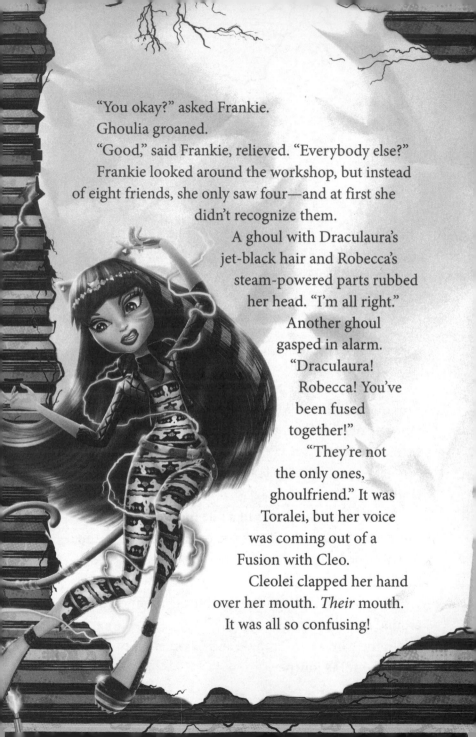

"You okay?" asked Frankie.

Ghoulia groaned.

"Good," said Frankie, relieved. "Everybody else?" Frankie looked around the workshop, but instead of eight friends, she only saw four—and at first she didn't recognize them.

A ghoul with Draculaura's jet-black hair and Robecca's steam-powered parts rubbed her head. "I'm all right."

Another ghoul gasped in alarm. "Draculaura! Robecca! You've been fused together!"

"They're not the only ones, ghoulfriend." It was Toralei, but her voice was coming out of a Fusion with Cleo.

Cleolei clapped her hand over her mouth. *Their* mouth. It was all so confusing!

Clawdeen was fused with Venus, Cleo was fused with Toralei, Lagoona Blue was fused with Jinafire, and Robecca was fused with Draculaura. They were all Fusions.

"This is soooooo freaky!" squealed Clawveenus.

"Oh. My. Ghoul!" Dracubecca shrieked.

Ghoulia and Frankie were the only two who were unchanged.

"How did this happen?" asked Dracubecca.

"I don't understand. Am I still Lagoona?"

"Or am I Jinafire?" asked the same ghoul.

Clawveenus sniffed. "I can smell *everything*!" Venus McFlytrap had to get used to having a werewolf nose.

Cleolei stamped her foot. "Ghoulia, how do we fix this? And don't say you don't know."

Ghoulia shrugged.

"Don't say that!" screeched Cleolei. "Of all the ghouls I could have been fused with, I end up with Toralei???"

Cleolei's left hand reached up and started honking her nose. Her right hand tried to wrestle it away from her face. The two hands were struggling with each other.

"I am still the queen of this body! You are just visiting," shouted the part of Cleolei that was Cleo.

Frankie intervened. "Everybody calm down. We can figure this out. That time teleport got us into this. I'm sure it can get us out."

But the teleporter looked hopelessly broken. The lens was crooked. The screwdriver was wedged into the gears. Everything was rusted.

"Somebody's just going to have to fix it," said Frankie, determined.

Everyone turned to Ghoulia, their eyes pleading with her to use her best spectral smarts to get them out of this fusion fiasco.

Ghoulia groaned, accepting the responsibility.

"Thank you!"

"We love you!"

"You're the best!"

She retrieved Hexiciah's journal. She had a lot of studying to do.

"So what do we do in the meantime?" asked Dracubecca.

Lagoonafire shrugged. "There's no sense in waiting around down here watching Ghoulia work."

"Should we go back upstairs for the rehearsal?" wondered Dracubecca.

"Sure," said Clawveenus sarcastically. "But what

are we gonna tell Mr. Where when he asks us how we got this way? We can't tell anybody about the time teleporter."

But they had to tell him *something*.

A little while later, in the auditorium, Mr. Where was trying to take it all in. "Your Mad Science Class assignment was to fuse yourselves together?"

The Fusions nodded in agreement.

"Works for me," said Mr. Where. "Okay, places, people, places! This play isn't going to rehearse itself!"

Clawveenus's nose wrinkled. "Did our going back in time somehow make his cologne stink get worse?"

The Venus part of Clawveenus chimed in. "Can I have my old nose back now?"

The ghouls headed backstage to begin the rehearsal while Mr. Where's glasses floated above a seat in the empty auditorium. He clapped his hands. "All right, thespians! Today is the day we travel back in time!"

Frankie had put on a long dress, just like the ones the ghouls had been wearing when she traveled back in time.

"And…action!" called out Mr. Where.

The lights dimmed. A monster fired up a spotlight and directed it toward the stage where Frankie was standing. Mr. Where clapped.

Frankie, who was the narrator for the production, began speaking. "For two hundred years, our great school has stood as a shining example of monster unity."

The Fusions, who had been passing by the auditorium, overheard her speech and stopped to listen.

"All monsters—the big, the small, the hairy, and the clawed," Frankie continued, "all are welcome to join our freaky family. Come with us now as we take a look back at Monster High—a *hissss*tory of exceptional acceptance."

Neighthan was beaming. "See? I told you Monster High is different," he whispered to the Fusions. He settled down in a seat in the back of the auditorium. The other Fusions reluctantly joined him.

The curtain opened and revealed a backdrop painted to show Monster High two hundred years ago. Students dressed in nineteenth-century bonnets and skirts wandered across the stage. Stagehands slid a cardboard cutout of a carriage, and a skeleton horse slid into place.

"Welcome to 1814!" announced Frankie. "Oh, what's that I see coming this way? Why, it's none other than Monster High's perpetual headmistress, our own Headless Headmistress Bloodgood!"

Cleolei, dressed like the headmistress, rode a prop Nightmare onto the stage. Behind her, Howleen and Twyla made horse noises.

In the back of the auditorium, the real Headmistress peeked in to watch the rehearsal. "Not bad!" she said.

But the real Nightmare was disappointed. He gave a grumpy neigh of disapproval before trotting away.

From the stage, Cleolei was delivering her lines. "Welcome, monsters, one and all. I declare Monster High officially open. May her walls ever stand as a beacon of hope and acceptance for *all* monsterkind."

Under her breath, Cleolei whispered, "And sorry about that cheap cologne smell. That would be our teacher, Mr. Where."

Howleen looked confused. "Is that the right line?"

"I don't think so," said Twyla.

Cleo and Toralei, two frenemies trapped in the same body, began bickering.

"Will you cut it out?"

"I don't know what you are talking about."

"This is hardly the time or place."

"Cut it out!"

Frankie cleared her throat, trying to get their attention.

"As I was saying," began Cleolei, returning to her lines. Unfortunately, Toralei was determined to make Cleo look ridiculous. Every time she opened her mouth to speak, she also began dancing. Suddenly, Cleolei began spinning around and around in circles as the fused ghouls fought with each other. Their arms flailed and they crashed into the Nightmare prop. It broke.

Frankie shook her head before trying to continue the rehearsal. "Everybody remembers the great zombie migration of 1845, when the first zombies arrived on our haunted shores."

Dracubecca came out on stage dressed as a fashionable ghoul in a hoopskirt. Deuce and Gil, acting like zombies, lumbered toward her.

"Where are your zombie costumes?" whispered Dracubecca.

"Buuuudget cuts," groaned Deuce in a zombie's moan.

"Gentle zombies!" Dracubecca acted. "Bring us your tired, your undead, your sluggish masses yearning to… Ahhhhhhh!"

Unexpectedly, Robecca's steam boots fired up and

propelled Dracubecca across the stage—headed right toward the zombies.

"Shuffle away," said Deuce, trying to avoid her.

"Shuffling," said Gil.

Dracubecca crashed into them with a scream.

Next up in the play was the war between the vampires and the werewolves. Stitched-together werewolf and vampire props were arranged in a battle scene. Lagoonafire stood in their midst.

"And did you know that Monster High played an integral role in the Werewolf-Vampire Reconciliation in the early twentieth century?" narrated Frankie.

"Werewolves, vampires, your scaritage makes no difference," proclaimed Lagoonafire. "All are welcome at Monster High!" She made a sweeping gesture with her arm but accidentally let loose a blast of dragon fire that ignited the werewolf props. They sizzled and burned.

"Oops!" said Lagoonafire, and more flames jetted from her hands, destroying the vampire soldiers. "Oops again!"

Hoodude, who'd been watching from backstage, covered his button eyes. "Oh no! I can't watch!"

In the back of the auditorium, the Fusions were mesmerized. Bonita was nervously chewing her clothes. "These ghouls need some serious help.

They're making me a nervous wreck."

Avia nodded in agreement. These monsters did not know how to handle being unexpected Fusions, that was for sure.

The stage had gone dark. When the spotlight turned on again, it found Gigi, Rochelle, and Clawveenus standing together, each holding a single red rose.

"Every monster is welcome at Monster High," said Gigi sweetly.

"Every monster is family at Monster High," sang Rochelle.

Clawveenus was about to deliver her lines when she began sneezing. "Achoo! Achoo!" The roses in the girls' hands grew bigger and bigger until they became a snarling and chomping rose

monster. Huge vines shot out of their stalks. One extended into the audience and coiled itself around Mr. Where.

Cleolei, still fighting with herself, tumbled back onstage.

"This is my body!"

"Cut it out!"

More flames erupted from Lagoonafire. Dracubecca flew across the stage on her steam boots, swirled into the rafters, knocked out a few lights, and crashed to the ground.

Frankie was at a loss for words.

Meanwhile, Sirena the Fusion had drifted over to the spotlight and was holding up her hands in front of it to create a monster shadow puppet onstage. She giggled.

Mr. Where, wrapped from head to toe in squeezing vines, was trying to remain positive. "All right. Good. Just a few notes."

But it was hopeless. Nobody was listening to him. The dress rehearsal had been a catastrophe.

Frankie went out to sit on the front steps of the school by herself, but she didn't realize that the

Fusions had followed her. They were watching her from behind a bush.

"Go talk to her," Avia said to Neighthan.

"I don't know," he said shyly.

Avia gave him a shove and he tumbled out of the bush and crashed—right in front of Frankie. He had twigs and leaves in his hair and he looked adorbs. "Um…hey…" he said awkwardly.

He brushed himself off and sat down beside Frankie. "That was some rehearsal back there."

"You saw, huh?"

He smiled. "Your friends gave some *fiery* performances."

Frankie chuckled.

"So what happened?" asked Neighthan.

"I'm not sure. An accident. They've all turned into, well, Fusions. And with two ghouls trying to operate in one body at the same time, they're having a lot of trouble keeping control of their powers. I'm really worried they might get hurt."

Neighthan nodded thoughtfully. "You must really care about them."

"So much," said Frankie. "And the thought of them

in trouble...I just get so emotional." A tiny spark shot out of her neck bolt and shocked Neighthan.

"Ow! What was that?"

"I'm not really sure," Frankie said apologetically. "It happens sometimes. Sorry."

They sat beside each other without speaking for a moment.

Finally, Neighthan broke the silence. Something had been on his mind since the rehearsal. "Did you ghouls really mean all that stuff you said onstage? About Monster High being like a family?"

"Everybody's welcome at Monster High," said Frankie. It was true. Everyone knew that.

Neighthan stood up, struggling to balance.

"Freaky flaws and all." Frankie smiled.

"Well, if that's really the case," said Neighthan, "I think we might be able to help your friends."

He offered Frankie his hand and helped her to her feet. Frankie blushed. He was such a gentleman.

"*We?*" she said shyly.

Avia, Bonita, and Sirena were peeking at them from behind the bush. Surprised, Bonita spread open her wings, and she bit down on her blouse.

"Do you think she sees us?" she whispered.

Avia sighed. She really needed some new friends.

THE MISSING MAD SCIENTIST

Back in Hexiciah's workshop, Ghoulia was trying to repair the broken teleporter. She had put on a welder's mask and gloves and was blasting the gears with a blowtorch. She checked out the control panel and caught a glance of herself in the reflection. Even in her gear, she was a glamorous ghoul.

She switched on the machine and it hummed. It began to whirr louder and louder and the gears started turning faster and faster. Ghoulia groaned in alarm.

BOOM!

The machine exploded in a cloud of smoke. Ghoulia was covered in soot.

She took off her gloves and her helmet, frustrated. It was back to the drawing board. She was going to have to do a lot more research in the library about Hexiciah.

Not long after she'd left the workshop, a thin blue flicker began to spark from the lens. The portal was opening. It flashed and disappeared and then flashed again.

BOOM!

The vortex opened with an explosion and out tumbled Sparky.

His hair was standing straight up and was now streaked in white from shock. His lab coat was in tatters. He looked disoriented.

"What happened?"

He noticed that the workshop was dirtier, older. He picked up Ghoulia's iCoffin, which she'd left on a bench. He began investigating it, and the phone's camera turned on and snapped a picture of him. The flash momentarily blinded him and he dropped it. When he recovered, he picked up the camera and was startled to see his own goofy face. "Fascinating!"

A monkey skeleton popped out of the clock and wheezed.

Sparky began pacing back and forth. "Aha!" he said, looking down at the phone in his hands. "This is the future, of course! I must not squander this opportunity. Who knows what futuristic technologies I can access. Perhaps this is where I will find the missing ingredient I need to finally create life!"

He pocketed the iCoffin and looked around the workshop for more modern gadgets. His eyes fell on Ghoulia's laptop and he picked it up. It was time to explore the future!

Ghoulia had picked up a smoothie while she was out doing research, and she was slurping it when she walked back into the workshop. It took her a moment to realize that everything was missing. Her iCoffin was gone. Her laptop was gone. Hexiciah's Recharge Chamber was missing. There were all kinds of missing tools and gadgets. Worst of all, the entire portal lens was gone. Ghoulia couldn't believe it. What had happened? Her smoothie splattered to the floor.

Tick, tick, tick. The clock on the door was moving. The time lock clicked, slammed, and closed. She would have to wait before she could open the door again. Ghoulia was trapped!

FUSIONS TO THE RESCUE!

Elsewhere in the catacombs, Neighthan was leading Frankie and the newly joined Fusions to the Fusions' secret underground lounge.

Dracubecca was very grateful. "It's so nice of you and the Fusions to offer your help...but it's not necessary," said the other part of her. "I think we're really getting the hang of this."

Dracubecca stopped walking and all of the other ghouls bumped into her. "We stopped. No, you stopped. After you. No, after you." Draculaura and Robecca were having a war of politeness—within the same body. It was just so confusing.

"No, you go ahead," said the part of Dracubecca that was Robecca. Her steam boots fired and knocked the Fusion off her feet. She crashed into the others and they all tumbled to the bottom of the stairs.

"Any help would be fangtastic," said Dracubecca to Neighthan.

A door opened in front of them into a small den-like room. It had an oozeball table, a vending machine, and comfortable couches. Torches flickered. Green vines stretched along the walls.

Bonita, Avia, and Sirena were huddled around a table, playing cards.

"Hey, Sirena," said Bonita. "Got any skulls?"

Sirena was balancing her cards on her head like a hat.

"Skulls, Sirena!" shrieked Avia, trying to get her attention.

Sirena jumped and the cards scattered. "Go squish," she said.

Avia noticed the new arrivals. "Hey, look, it's the new combos. You ghouls put on one heckuva show this afternoon."

"Frankie and friends," introduced Neighthan, "I'd like you to meet Avia Trotter—part harpy and part centaur."

Avia nodded.

"Bonita Femur," said Neighthan. "Skeleton-moth." Bonita chewed on her blouse nervously.

Finally, Neighthan introduced Sirena. "Mermaid-ghost."

"You ghouls gotta check out this bug crawling on the wall," said Sirena, distracted as usual.

"We're all Fusions," said Neighthan.

"And what makes you think you'll be able to help us?" asked Clawveenus. She emitted a haze of pollen and sneezed.

"Because we're Fusions and you're Fusions now, and we all have our freaky flaws to deal with," explained Neighthan. "Like Bonita. She's… jumpy. And Sirena. She's a free spirit."

"Go, little guy! Go!" said Sirena to the bug on the wall.

"And Avia," continued Neighthan. "Avia—"

"Interrupts a lot," interrupted Avia.

"Right," said Neighthan. "Anyway, we understand what

you're going through. And we want to help."

Cleolei wasn't so sure. "Fusions being nice? Are you sure we came back to the right timeline?"

"Listen," said Avia. "We're sorry we gave you ghouls the cold shoulder before."

Bonita nodded in agreement. "We've had so many bad experiences with the monsters at our other schools. We just don't trust anyone anymore, ya know?"

"Monster High is different," Frankie assured her. "We're all a family, and now you're part of it."

Avia looked uncertain. "We'll see…"

Lagoonafire was staring at Neighthan. "You didn't tell us any of *your* freaky flaws."

He looked uncomfortable. "Who, me? Well, I get some healing powers from my unicorn side. But my zombie side makes me…what would I call it?"

He walked across the lounge and accidentally put his leg into a small trash can. He tripped, flew forward, waved his arms to steady himself, and crashed into the vending machine. It clinked like a slot machine and snacks began pouring out of it.

"I'm clumsy," Neighthan admitted.

Frankie couldn't help but smile. He was totes adorbs!

CHAPTER 15

SPOOKY SELFIES

Sparky was experimenting in a secret laboratory. A coil sparked with electricity. He had created an elaborate device involving the Recharge Chamber, the iCoffin, the laptop, and the teleporter lens all connected by a tangle of wires that led to a giant mound underneath a white sheet.

Sparky typed a set of instructions into the laptop. He texted on the iCoffin. He laughed maniacally.

The iCoffin camera flashed and knocked him over. He rubbed his eyes and checked out his accidental photo. "Looking pretty good in this one! Now, where was I? Oh yes!" He cackled.

What was he up to?

CHAPTER 16

MONSTER MAKEOVERS

Frankie was hurrying down the hallway when Mr. Rotter stopped her.

"I trust you're making progress on your revised scaritage report for tomorrow?" he said.

Frankie panicked and recovered. "So, so much progress," she lied. "It's scary."

Mr. Rotter narrowed his eyes. "You'd better be. Or it's going to be lights-out for your scaremester average!"

As if on cue, the hallway lights flickered. Something was up with the electrical current somewhere in the school.

"Not my doing," said Mr. Rotter, somewhat startled. "But helpful for making my point." He headed toward his classroom, while Frankie ran to the gym to meet up with the Fusions.

In the gym, Avia had lined everyone up. The Fusions and the new Fusions were all standing at attention like soldiers while Avia, her wings spread and fluttering, addressed them.

"All right, ghouls, listen up. We're going to pair each of you with a Fusion mentor to help you master your new combined forms. But before we get started, I'd like you to think about this." Avia held up a coin.

"Money? Way ahead of you," squealed Cleo.

"She's about to use it as a metaphor, Your Highness," said Toralei.

"Don't make me come over there, Miss Kitty."

"I'd like to see you try!"

This entire squabble was happening within the fused body of Cleolei. Avia whinnied to get their attention.

"A coin has two sides," continued Avia, fluttering back and forth along the ranks. "Like you. And no matter what, you can't have one side without the other. So you're going to have to get along."

She flipped the coin over to Cleolei. Both of her hands began fighting the other to hold it.

"I'm keeping this!"

"It's mine!"

Dracubecca felt dizzy. "I don't know if I can do this. It's like my brain tells me to do one thing, but something inside makes me do something else." One of her steam boots fired and she toppled over. "Ow!"

Neighthan helped her up. "That's because you're getting mixed signals. That's Draculaura's mind getting confused by Robecca's instincts. With a little practice, you'll figure out when to listen to what's up *here*," he said, pointing to his head, "and what's in *here*." Neighthan pointed at his heart.

What Neighthan said reminded Frankie of something she'd heard in Hexiciah's class. "The spark," she whispered to herself.

"Okay," announced Avia in full training mode. "Who's ready to get to work?"

Dracubecca raised her hand.

"Good. I like your spirit, kid."

Dracubecca looked at her raised hand, alarmed. "I had no idea I was doing that!"

Avia shook her head. It was going to be a long afternoon.

Bonita took Clawveenus into the garden and had

her sit with her legs crossed, in the lotus position, to begin to calm her mind. "I've been fluttering from school to school ever since I was just a little larvette," Bonita told Clawveenus. "It was always really tough, but I found that meditation would clear my head and make me feel in control. And I think it can help you too."

"It's worth a shot!" agreed Clawveenus, shutting her eyes the way Bonita had instructed her.

"Now clear your mind," said the skeleton-moth.

"And clear." Clawveenus sighed.

"Now take a deep, soothing breath."

Clawveenus inhaled and started sneezing and snorting. Her lungs were filled with pollen again.

A plant behind her began to sprout vines. One of them inched forward, wrapped itself around Bonita, and flung her into the air. Bonita spread her wings and swooped toward the plant like an action hero, beating it back.

Her eyes shut, Clawveenus had no idea what was happening. "Hey, I think it's working! I feel totally in control!"

In the Fusion lounge, Cleolei was lying on one of the couches like she was in a psychiatrist's office. Neighthan was sitting in a chair beside her taking notes.

"So you're saying that you're going to make Toralei and me get along with each other by…talking? Good luck with that!"

"No, it's true," said Neighthan. "I've spent a lot of time in school counselors' offices just talking through what it's like to be a Fusion. I promise, talking really helps."

"All right, Toralei, let's talk."

"All right, Toralei, let's talk," mimicked Toralei.

"Real mature," said Cleo.

"Real mature," repeated Toralei. She screeched like a cat and Cleolei's two hands began swatting at each other again.

"Why don't you take this seriously?"

"You're not the boss of me!"

Neighthan sighed. "I guess technically they're talking…" But he didn't hold out much hope that it was going to make any difference at all.

While the Fusions were trying to help the Fusions, Sparky was sneaking around Monster High collecting materials for his experiment. He made sure no one was coming down the hallway and slipped into the science classroom. A few minutes later, he emerged with a stack of beakers in his hands and one carefully balanced on his head, chortling to himself.

Next, he slunk into the Creepateria. While Manny, Gil, and Deuce chatted at one of the tables, Sparky reached up from below and grabbed each of their iCoffins.

Ghoulia was still locked in Hexiciah's workshop, unable to get out. She kept checking her watch, but the time was moving so slowly.

In the gym, Avia had set up an obstacle course of tires, ropes, and hurdles for Dracubecca. "I've learned that surviving as a Fusion means that you have to take charge," she explained. "And from what I've seen, your problem is that neither of you is taking charge of your body. You're both too polite."

"Right. I'll let Robecca take the lead."

"No, it should really be Draculaura."

"That's so sweet. But I really do insist that—"

"All right, all right," interrupted Avia. "See? That's what I'm talking about. I don't care who it is, but somebody has to be the leader. Now, let's give it a try."

Avia flew up into the air to watch Dracubecca navigate the obstacle course. She clicked a stopwatch. "Go!"

Dracubecca's steam boots rocketed her into the course. *Crash! Bash! Smash!* The obstacle course was in pieces. Avia clicked the stopwatch. Dracubecca poked her head up through the wreckage. Avia was not amused.

Meanwhile, Sparky had snuck into the boys' restroom with a ladder and was carefully unscrewing lightbulbs. The bathroom went black.

"Hello? Hello?" called Heath from one of the stalls.

At the school pool, Sirena was trying to help Lagoonafire, but she was having a hard time focusing. "So, like, the ghost side of my family never really got along with the mermaid side. But there was always one activity that could bring both families together…" Her voice trailed off and she stared vacantly at the water.

Lagoonafire waited. And waited. And waited. "Swimming?" she finally asked.

Sirena brightened. "Sure! I love swimming!" She rose into the air and executed four perfect backward somersaults before slipping into the water without a splash.

Lagoonafire was impressed. "Crikey! I've never seen anybody pull off a quadruple reverse somersault without splashing! That was gorgeous!"

"Like I said." Sirena smiled. "We did a lot of swimming in my family."

"All right, Jinafire, you ready, mate?"

"Are you sure this is wise?"

"Trust me. A good swim is just what we need to let off a little steam."

When both parts of Lagoonafire were in agreement, she dove deep into the water. The pool began to bubble and hiss and steam. In an instant, all of the water had evaporated. Lagoonafire was sitting at the bottom of an empty pool. "Too much steam." She sighed.

Could a dragon girl and a mermaid ever learn to live together as one? It was probably as likely as a werecat and a mummy princess getting along!

Yet, somehow, Cleo and Toralei were learning how to talk to each other. Cleolei's head turned this way and that, her mouth kept moving, and the words poured out—but they were less and less irritated. Neighthan couldn't believe that they were having an actual discussion.

Avia had set up the obstacle course again, and this time Dracubecca was carefully making her way through it. As the Fusion crossed the finish line, Avia clicked her stopwatch and nodded with approval. Not bad, not bad at all.

In the garden, Clawveenus and Bonita were doing gentle yoga postures. Around them, flowers blossomed—but not a single one turned into a plant monster.

Even Lagoonafire was learning to control her powers. The pool had been refilled and Sirena watched delightedly as Lagoonafire dove gracefully in and out of the water. Each time she emerged, she sent a controlled blaze of flame through a hoop suspended from the ceiling. Lagoonafire sailed into the air, dove through the burning hoop, and landed on the ground. "Ta-da!" she announced. Sirena beamed with pride and went to hug her but became distracted by a shiny whistle. Sirena grabbed it, blew it, and startled a sleepy gargoyle lifeguard.

Back in the Fusion lounge, everyone was celebrating. The Fusions had learned how to control themselves! Clawveenus was drawing in her sketchbook and Cleolei was happily recounting their time-travel adventures to the Fusions.

"So there we are, stranded, all one in the year 1814 thanks to Touchy McPoke-at-Stuff." Cleolei pointed to herself. "And guess what she goes and does next?"

"Don't tell me she wandered off on her own!" exclaimed Avia.

"I wandered off on my own!" admitted Cleolei. Everyone laughed.

"It's like that old saying," suggested Dracubecca. "*Fusions make the best teachers.*"

Avia looked confused. "That's not an old saying."

"Oh, well, it should be." Dracubecca smiled. She fired up her steam boots, twirled in the air, and landed gracefully—although the steam did extinguish a couple of the torches. "Oops!"

"No worries, love," said Lagoonafire reassuringly. She blew a controlled flame across the room and relit them.

All the Fusions clapped.

"Yeah, yeah, show-off." Clawveenus laughed. She set down her sketchbook and closed her eyes. For a moment, nothing seemed to be happening. But vines on the walls sprouted the most beautiful flowers.

"Oooh!"

"Awww!"

"Very impressive!"

"Nice touch!"

Clawveenus was proud of herself. "Who's got two green thumbs and a room full of freaky Fusion friends?" She pointed at herself. "This ghoul right here!"

Neighthan drifted across the room to a passageway that overlooked a massive underground cavern. Frankie was there, leaning against a rock. Beneath them ran a glowing river of lava, lit up by beams of the setting sun shining through cracks in the rock. It was romantic—in a creepy kind of way.

"The lava is really quite lovely this time of day," Neighthan remarked.

Frankie smiled, her thoughts far away. "Yeah."

"If you're still worried about your friends, you shouldn't be. They're going to be great tonight."

"Thanks to you," said Frankie. "No, I was thinking about something else. Something you said made me think about my grandfather. And how much I really don't know about him. Or myself."

"What do you mean?"

Frankie turned to Neighthan, pointing at her head. "I know I have this, but do I have this?" She touched her heart. "Professor Steam said you needed more than just spare parts to create a life. You need something inside—he called it a spark. So what did Victor Frankenstein discover that gave life to me? If I was built in some laboratory, am I even really alive at all? What if I'm just...parts?"

"That's some heavy stuff," acknowledged Neighthan. "You sure you don't want to go back to small talk about the slime?"

"I'm sorry," said Frankie with an apologetic smile. "This whole scaritage project has put a lot of questions between my bolts. I just wish I could talk to my grandfather."

Neighthan rested his hand over hers. Sometimes a touch said more than words. Frankie looked up into his eyes. Sparks jolted from her neck bolts, electrifying Neighthan and knocking him backward. Startled bats swooped across the cavern.

"Neighthan, I'm so sorry!"

Steam rose from Neighthan's hand, but he was grinning. "You know how you know you're alive? You can feel it. Did you feel that?"

Frankie nodded.

"Me too!" said Neighthan, rubbing his hand. "But hey, now we know you're really alive. Maybe that was the spark your professor was talking about."

If Frankie had looked a little more carefully, she would have seen, across the cavern, the time-clock door to Hexiciah's workshop. Ghoulia was still stuck there waiting for the hour when it would open. She'd used the spare time to curl her hair, using stray bottles and dowels to give her ghostly white locks a lift.

Tick, tick, tick. Finally it was time for the door to open! Ghoulia pulled out her bottle rollers, gave her hair a toss, and dashed out the door. If she were lucky, she'd make it just in time for the bite-centennial celebration.

Monsters were pouring into the auditorium for the big night. Lightning flashed. Thunder rumbled in the distance. Searchlights lit up the big bite-centennial banner. It was almost showtime!

Headmistress Bloodgood galloped through the auditorium on Nightmare. "Happy bite-centennial, Monster High. Take your seats! Take your seats!"

The audience was filled with eager students, teachers, and parents holding cameras. Backstage, the actors were putting last-minute touches to their makeup. Frankie peeked through the curtain at the crowd.

"It's a full house, ghouls," Mr. Where said anxiously. "You're sure we're not going to have a repeat of this afternoon's rehearsal?"

Dracubecca hovered on her steam boots. "You can count on us!" The Fusions waved at her, confident that she could do it.

The stage lights flickered and buzzed. Mr. Where looked more concerned than ever. "No, no, no. This play cannot be ruined by technical difficulties! I'd never be able to show my face again." Of course, no one had ever actually seen Mr. Where's face.

He stomped off to investigate what was going wrong electrically.

Ghoulia emerged from the catacombs and rushed toward the school. Panting and out of breath, she burst through the stage door.

"There you are!" said Clawveenus. "Hey, your hair looks claw-some."

Ghoulia smiled and touched one of her new curls, but then she gave a serious series of groans.

"You figured out how to separate us!" exclaimed Lagoonafire. "That's great! The show's about to start."

"Ooooooooooo!" moaned Ghoulia. It wasn't that easy.

"Part of the time teleporter lens was stolen?" Cleolei translated. "How?"

"Maybe we can, I don't know, buy another time lens?" suggested Dracubecca, but when everybody glared at her, she realized what a ridiculous idea that was. "No, you're right. That's crazy. No time lens store is going to be open at this hour."

Ghoulia was increasingly frustrated.

"This doesn't make any sense," said Frankie. "Who would steal the time lens? What's going on?"

The stage lights buzzed and dimmed again. It was almost as if something was interfering with the electrical current.

Hidden in his laboratory, Sparky was hard at work. Power nodes were firing, coils were glowing, and the light meters were zapping at full capacity. Sparky was wearing giant black goggles while he dashed around throwing switches and twisting dials. Beakers bubbled and steamed. Everything was centered on the giant mound covered by the white sheet.

"This is it! This is going to happen! I'm finally going to have a family!" Sparky cackled.

He threw the master switch, and the laboratory exploded with electricity. The figure under the sheet jolted and began shaking violently. An enormous arm flopped out. It started to twitch.

"It's alive! It's alive!" screamed Sparky. "I really hope it's alive. It's so embarrassing when it's not alive."

Slowly, the giant Creature slid its legs off the table. It threw off the sheet. It stood up on its own two feet.

It *was* alive—and it was enormous!

"Rrrrrrrrrr!" it roared.

Sparky was thrilled beyond belief. "Excellent! Now just a few more programming commands and Genealogi-bot 4.0 will be finished! And then the two of us will be…doing whatever it is families do—in no time!"

Sparky rushed over to the tangle of computers and phones connected to the Recharge Chamber. He typed furiously and then moved to another keyboard. "Yes, yes, executing the family algorithm, applying the genealogy coefficient…" His hands darted from device to device. He picked up an iCoffin—and once again set off the camera. *Flash!*

Temporarily blinded, Sparky clutched one of the keyboards to steady himself. Without even realizing it, he was typing a string of random letters. An accidental code began entering into the computer program. Sparky bashed his hand onto the laptop in anger. Red warning lights flashed on the screen.

"All right," said Sparky, breathing heavily. "Now I just have to upload…Success…" He clicked a button. "Manners." He clicked another button. He took off his goggles and turned toward his creation.

"You are my family," he told the Creature.

It responded in a programmed, mechanical voice that was a lot like Sparky's. "Fa-mi-ly."

"Yes!" Sparky jumped up and down. "It works! I created life! I knew I was just missing something before, but I've found the missing ingredient!" Tears welled up in his eyes. "I want to remember this moment forever. Wait! I know!"

Sparky grabbed one of the iCoffins, dragging along wires and computers. He focused on his Creature. "Say…artificially intelligent family member constructed in a lab!"

He clicked the camera. *Flash!*

The Creature blinked rapidly and its body began emitting an eerie red light. A warning code flashed on one of the computer screens. "Rahhh!" it screamed. "Bad! Blinded by science!"

Its flailing arms threw Sparky across the lab. He crashed into the Recharge Chamber. *Smash! Bash! Crash!* The Creature staggered toward the door. It pulled the door off its hinges. It was stomping down the tower stairs—toward the high school.

"No, you can't go!" screamed Sparky. "You're supposed to stay here with me!"

But it was too late. The Creature was already gone.

ATTACK OF THE CREATURE

Backstage, the ghouls were trying to figure out what to do about the lost lens. There was no way to fix the Fusions without it.

Dracubecca was upset. "Without a time teleporter, does that mean we're Fusions forever?"

Cleolei flipped. "I can't be stuck with Toralei for the rest of my life!"

"I thought you two were getting along now," said Clawveenus.

Cleolei stamped her foot. "That was then, this is now. There were zombie-corns, flying horse ghouls, I got confused."

Mr. Where's glasses peeked backstage. "Showtime, people!" He ushered Frankie toward the front of the auditorium. The house lights were dimming. The audience was quieting down. Everyone applauded when Frankie stepped in front of the curtain.

This is going to be some acting job, thought Frankie. She smiled and waved. "Um…hi!"

There was dead silence in the audience. From one of the back seats came the shy voice of Neighthan. "Hi, Frankie!" he called.

Frankie took a deep breath. "For two hundred years, our great school has stood as a shining example of monster unity. All monsters—the big, the small, the hairy, and the clawed—are welcome."

At that exact moment, a giant arm thrust itself through the stage floor right in front of Frankie. It was the Creature! Frankie let loose a bloodcurdling scream! The audience couldn't figure out if this was part of the show or not.

The Creature smashed through the floorboards and emerged. It was a terrifying mishmash of computers, phones, and plain old junk. Its face was a laptop screen with an image of a face projected onto it. It had giant bolts on its shoulders and a license plate on its butt. This wasn't a living creature—it was a technological construction. Where its heart should be was the giant time-machine lens.

The disoriented Creature blinked under the stage lights. It turned toward the audience. "Fa-mi-ly!" it roared.

Students and their parents screamed and rushed toward the exits.

Iris turned to Manny. "I think it's time to go."

"I think you're right," said Manny, getting up.

"Where are you going?" asked Heath. "The play is just getting good." He ducked as the Creature ripped out an auditorium chair and hurled it over his head. "Ahhh!" He followed his friends as fast as he could.

Everyone was fleeing from the rampaging Creature.

"Destroy! Rah!" it shrieked.

Backstage, the ghouls were horrified.

"What *is* that thing?" wondered Clawveenus.

Ghoulia recognized the time teleporter lens on its chest. She groaned, trying to explain to the others what she'd seen.

Out of the hole in the stage clambered Sparky. He was out of breath. "Okay...here I come...Just...stop..."

"Sparky!" Frankie recognized him.

He stopped, a guilty expression on his face.

Frankie couldn't believe it. "You followed us through the time portal? Just so you could build... that?"

"You say that like it's a bad thing," he said defensively.

The Creature ripped out another chair.

Sparky laughed nervously. "It's okay. There's just

something wrong with its programming. I can fix it…I think…"

Cleolei pulled out her iCoffin and took a photo of the Creature for her Fearbook profile. But the flash made the Creature furious. Its eyes flashed red.

"Yeah," said Sparky sheepishly. "It doesn't like that."

The angry Creature charged the stage. It knocked Sparky aside and grabbed Cleolei. Like King Kong, it lifted her into the air.

"Put me down!" ordered Cleolei.

"No, put *me* down," said the part of Cleolei that was Toralei.

The Creature held Cleolei close to its chest, which somehow activated the time portal lens. The swirling blue vortex appeared, exerting its magnetic pull. Cleolei felt herself being pulled closer and closer—until it sucked her inside! She was trapped! The ghouls could see her hovering behind the lens. She was even angrier than the Creature.

"I did not see that coming," admitted Sparky.

"Ugh! Gross!" shrieked Cleolei from inside the portal. "Let us out of here!"

"Rahhhhhh!" roared the Creature as it lurched and stumbled out of the auditorium.

Frankie was stunned. "That thing just absorbed my friends."

"That *thing*," Sparky corrected her, "is Geneologi-bot 4.0."

Clawveenus smacked Sparky on the side of his head.

"Ow!" He rubbed the sore spot. "I guess I didn't find the ingredient that creates life. It must realize something is missing and is trying to replace it."

Clawveenus smacked Sparky again.

"*Ow!*"

"How do we shut it down?" asked Frankie. They could hear it rampaging through the hallways of Monster High. There was no telling what it was doing.

"Shut it down?" Sparky couldn't believe it. "You can't! It's my family!"

Frankie, who was normally very gentle, grabbed Sparky by the collar of his shirt. "You *have* a family, Sparky. And they're out there running for their lives from the thing you created. *We're* your family. And Professor Steam. Monster High is your family."

"And we're part of it," said Neighthan, appearing at Frankie's side.

"Look around!" Frankie ordered Sparky. "Is this what you had in mind when you built that monster?"

The auditorium was destroyed. The curtain was ripped. The floor was smashed. The chairs had been ripped out. Sparky was trying to take it all in. "You don't understand," he said at last.

Neighthan shook his head and turned to Frankie. "What can we do to help?"

"I don't know," said Frankie. "You'll have to ask Sparky."

Sparky was slumped to the ground, holding his head in his hands. He looked up at the monsters standing around him. "You really see yourselves as a family?"

Frankie nodded. "Freaky flaws and all."

A light seemed to turn on inside of Sparky. "You're right. We have to stop this." He got up and started pacing back and forth, brainstorming. "I brought it to life with electricity. I suppose a large-enough blast of energy of opposing polarity might stop it."

Ghoulia had something to moan about all of this.

"Yes," agreed Sparky. "Hexiciah's Recharge Chamber! That could work. But we have to lead the Creature to my lab in the catacombs. It's in the security room behind the time lock."

Frankie took charge. "All right, then. Ghoulia,

you and Sparky head down to the lab and prep the charging chamber. The rest of us will figure out a way to lead the Creature down to the catacombs."

Ghoulia and Sparky hurried out, and Frankie and the Fusions geared themselves up to tackle the Creature. Screams echoed from somewhere in Monster High. Sirena looked distracted and a little lost.

"All right, ghouls, let's do this," urged Frankie.

"Let's do this," echoed Sirena, not entirely sure what she was saying.

The Creature was trudging down the hallway, smashing its fist into the lockers. It was crushing fountains, pulling down candelabras, and destroying everything in its path. Floating inside the time portal lens, Cleolei watched the chaos unfold.

"It took getting absorbed by a giant gross-smelling Creature, but I finally realize there are worse things than being fused with you, Toralei," said Cleo.

"Aww, that's really sweet," said Toralei, touched.

The Creature let out an enormous burp as it bashed its way toward the main entry, ripping down bite-centennial banners.

"We can't let it leave the school," said Frankie, alarmed.

"A little steam power if you will, love?" Lagoonafire stepped onto Dracubecca's feet. She activated her boots and the two Fusions blasted down the hallway. Lagoonafire laid a trail of flames behind them as they swooped past the front door that blocked the Creature from leaving.

"Raaa!" it roared. It recoiled from the fire.

"It doesn't look happy," said Dracubecca. But they were too close to it—and the blue vortex was beginning to pull them in.

"Hold on to something!" yelled Clawveenus.

But it was too late. Lagoonafire and Dracubecca were sucked into the lens with Cleolei.

"No!" screamed Frankie.

"Raaa!" roared the Creature, charging past the ghouls into the hallways of Monster High.

Clawveenus watched it rampage. "Okay, how are we going to get that thing to go to the catacombs? Because I don't think asking nicely is an option."

Frankie took out her iCoffin and studied it. "I've got an idea. Everybody meet me at the door to the catacombs in the hallway."

"I'm coming with you," said Neighthan gallantly.

"No, I've got this," said Frankie. "I'm not letting anyone else get sucked into that thing."

Down in Sparky's lab, Ghoulia watched while the

teenage mad scientist tore open a panel on Hexiciah's Recharge Chamber. "Let's see...polarity, polarity," he muttered to himself. He reached in to cut a wire and stopped. Then he reached for a different wire. He hesitated. Ghoulia grabbed the wire cutters from him and pushed him out of the way. Immediately, she began rewiring the chamber. Sparky was impressed.

But there wasn't any time to lose.

The Creature clomped through the hallways, growling and destroying lockers. It turned a corner, and there, standing right in front of it, was Frankie.

She held up her iCoffin. "Smile!"

Flash!

The light hit the Creature. It blinked and recoiled.

Frankie took a quick look at the photo. "Ugh. I'd say I got your bad side, but I'm not sure there's a good one."

The Creature had recovered and seen Frankie. "That's right," she encouraged it. "You...Whatever... It's hard to find the right word...This way!" She turned and ran, and it followed her.

Mr. Rotter chose that moment to pop out of his classroom. "Frankie Stein!" he shouted, displeased. "Your assignment was to complete your scaritage report, and instead I find you running through the halls?" He flipped his pencil into the air and caught it.

Frankie glanced around nervously. Where was the Creature? "Um…Mr. Rotter…" she began.

But before she could explain what was happening, there was an enormous crash. "Rahhhhh!" bellowed the Creature. Mr. Rotter jumped into the air and dropped his pencil.

"Your friend makes a good point." Mr. Rotter gulped, quickly stepping back inside the classroom and shutting the door.

Frankie took off—but she was running so quickly, she tripped on her platform shoes and fell to the floor.

"Graahhh!" The Creature's shadow loomed over Frankie. She screamed.

"I'll save you, Frankie!" Neighthan charged down the hallway. He fell to his knees, heroically careering to the rescue like a baseball player sliding into home plate. Unfortunately, he whizzed past Frankie and crashed into an empty classroom.

"I'm okay," he called, emerging with a wastebasket over his head. He pulled it off, threw it aside, and grabbed Frankie's hand. He pulled her into his arms and whisked her away from the Creature at the very last minute. "When we get back to the others, can we skip telling them that part about the trash can?"

"My hero!" Frankie sighed, wrapping her arms around Neighthan's neck. Her bolts sparked and sizzled.

But the Creature was dangerously close. It was stomping toward them, getting closer and closer. It was about to get them when Sirena hovered in front of it, distracting it from Frankie.

"Hey, look here!" she sang in her haunting voice. She wafted across the hallway. "Now look here!"

The beast, confused, paused. "Rahh?"

"Now look at this!" she trilled. She flew graceful circles around the beast's head, leaving a glowing trail of ghostly haze.

"Be careful, Sirena!" Frankie warned. Neighthan was galloping away with her in his arms.

As they ran, Bonita and Avia hovered along beside them.

"Avia! Bonita!" Frankie was thrilled to see them both.

"Looks like you two could use a lift!" said Avia.

Both of the Fusions grabbed one of Neighthan's arms and slowly lifted the couple into the air to safety.

20

FRANKIE'S SPECIAL SPARK

Clawveenus, Frankie, and the Fusions raced through the door to the catacombs. Operetta was practicing her organ, oblivious to the mayhem happening above her. She barely looked up as the ghouls ran past her, the Creature in hot pursuit. Finally, almost out of breath, they arrived at the laboratory.

"Did you get him to follow you?" asked Sparky. But before they could answer, the Creature roared. Sparky gulped. "Okay, then."

"I think it's time for a little di-*vine* intervention," said Clawveenus. She closed her eyes and raised her arms. Enormous vines pierced the walls of the laboratory, squiggled toward the Creature, and shackled its arms and feet. It struggled to free itself but couldn't—but it reached out its hand and grabbed Clawveenus. It pulled her into the lens with the other ghouls!

"No!" screamed Frankie.

Avia and Bonita both grabbed a thick jumper cable, flew up into the air, and attached them to the bolts on the Creature's shoulders.

"Do it now!" Frankie commanded.

Ghoulia hit a switch on the Recharge Chamber, unleashing a wave of electricity that traveled through the cables and blasted into the Creature. But it wasn't a strong-enough current. The Creature ripped its arm loose from the vines.

"It's not working," declared Sparky. "There's not enough energy."

With its free arm, the Creature yanked out the electrical wires from the Recharge Chamber. Sparks exploded like fireworks. The machine smoked, hissed, and died. The Creature struggled to free itself from the vines.

"Frankie! Help us!" pleaded the ghouls trapped inside the lens.

"How could you do this?" Frankie yelled at Sparky. Tears were streaming down her cheeks. "Those are my friends!" She marched right up to the Creature. "You took my friends from me! The ones I love!" The bolts on Frankie's neck sparked. "Do you have any idea how that makes me *feel*?"

"What's happening?" asked Sparky, noticing the flashes of electricity coming from Frankie.

"I've seen that before," said Neighthan. "It's her spark."

Frankie was so filled with emotion that electricity was pouring through her body. "The sparks," she realized. All of a sudden, she unscrewed her neck bolts, swapping them to opposite sides. She marched over to the jumper cables still connected to the Creature's shoulders, picked them up, and clamped them to her neck.

"No, Frankie!" screamed Dracubecca. "It's too dangerous!"

But it was too late.

"Give me back my friends!" shouted Frankie with her whole heart. Her body lit up with sparks of blue light that streamed toward the Creature.

"I don't understand," said Sparky. "It's just electricity."

"No," Neighthan corrected him. "It's something else. It's her spark—her emotions, her life force. It's… her!"

The Creature was resisting Frankie's life force, trying to send out dark matter to squash the spark.

Sparky, watching the battle between the animated pile of junk he'd created and the ghoul filled with courage and passion, realized something at last. "She's everything my creation isn't. The spark. That's what makes her alive. That's what I've been missing. Professor Steam was right."

The Creature flailed wildly, breaking free from another vine.

Frankie was concentrating, sending more and more of her life force through the cables. The Creature stumbled backward. It fell. The vortex opened and Cleo and Toralei clambered out of the lens.

"What happened?" said Cleo, looking at her restored body. "I'm…I'm me again."

Knowing that her efforts were saving her friends,

Frankie focused her energy with even greater power, intensifying the current. Lagoona and Jinafire were free.

"Frankie, you saved us!"

Ghoulia groaned, explaining how their journey through the lens was restoring their original forms.

Frankie's hair was standing on end, her stitches were beginning to loosen, and an explosion of sparks was flying out of her. Clawdeen and Venus climbed out of the lens, separated. But Frankie was on her knees. She had nothing left.

"I have to save Draculaura and Robecca," she whispered.

"You can't take any more," said Jinafire.

Frankie struggled to her feet as the Creature ripped its legs free from the vines. It roared and charged toward the ghouls. But Frankie wasn't going to let it hurt them. She still had something left. A massive wave of energy exploded out of her, blasted through the cables, and poured into the Creature. For a moment, it stopped, frozen. An error message started blinking on the laptop screen that was its face. Draculaura and Robecca fell out of the open portal.

The Creature was still. Ghoulia walked over to it, tapped it with her finger, and it crashed to the floor. A few last pieces of equipment—a cell phone here, a laptop there—flickered for a moment or two before dying out.

It was over. Frankie had defeated it. They were all safe.

Except for Frankie.

She was lying on the ground with her eyes closed. She wasn't moving—at all.

"Oh, Frankie," said Lagoona, bending close. "What did you do?"

"She saved us," whispered Venus. "She saved all of us."

Frankie's eyelashes fluttered.

Draculaura rushed over. "Frankie! Come back to us! Wake up!"

Sparky pushed his way through the ghouls to Frankie. He kneeled down close beside her and gently took her hand. "This is all my fault. I should have listened to Professor Steam—and not forced the creation of life before I understood it. Before you showed me that there really is something…in here." He touched his heart as tears spilled out of his eyes.

"And now you've gone and used up all your spark. To save your friends."

Frankie's mouth was moving. Her voice was faint. "To save my friends." She was fading. "I told you it was possible to create life. Just like my grandfather did so many years ago. Just like Victor Frankenstein."

Sparky's eyes widened. "My name is Victor Frankenstein."

The ghouls were shocked. This normie boy who'd caused so much trouble was the great inventor?

Sparky gulped. He hardly knew what to say. "I'm your grandfather," he whispered to Frankie.

A faint smile turned up the corners of her lips. "Sparky's your nickname."

He nodded.

"So I got to meet my grandfather...after...all..." Her eyes closed. A last gentle breath disappeared from her mouth. Frankie was gone.

The ghouls and the Fusions were devastated. They held one another and cried. They barely spoke. No one knew what to say. Their beloved Frankie was gone. How could it be?

"Without her, we'd all still be part of that... Creature," said Clawdeen at last.

"It doesn't seem real." Even Cleo was weeping, although carefully so as not to smudge her eye makeup.

Neighthan wiped away a tear.

Ghoulia was sad too, but she was also thinking. Something had occurred to her. She pulled Sparky aside.

"No!" he said. "You don't mean..."

Ghoulia nodded and groaned some more.

"You're right," said Sparky, brightening. "That just might work. But we have to get the polarity just right."

Ghoulia offered some more suggestions.

"Okay, I understand zombie," whispered Toralei. "But I have no idea what any of this means."

"It means," said Sparky, jumping up, "that we're going to save Frankie!"

"What?"

"You can't be serious!"

"You really think you can bring her back?" Robecca was stunned.

Cleo looked uncertain. "Tell us you're not trying to be funny."

"The only funny thing happening right now," said Sparky, "is that that mermaid-ghost is paying zero attention to this conversation."

Sirena had drifted across the laboratory and was staring at an arc of electricity that was still sparking. "Pretty!" she said, reaching out to touch it.

Sparky shook his head. "We can do this. But not in here. This place is a mess."

"Gee," said Clawdeen with her usual tough-girl honesty. "I wonder what could have caused that."

Sparky grimaced, embarrassed. "Just help me gather supplies and we'll bring Frankie back to

Professor Steam's workshop."

The ghouls and Fusions were energized by Sparky's optimism, but Ghoulia was studying the Recharge Chamber. It was dented and blackened. Would it still work?

Sparky shared her concern. "This Recharge Chamber is going to need a little love…"

Ghoulia groaned in agreement.

Working together, the ghouls and the Fusions managed to move everything back to Hexiciah's workshop. They polished instruments, hammered out dents, and repaired wires. The time portal lens was back in place between the magnets. Cleo and Toralei even gave the Recharge Chamber a fresh coat of paint. The only question that remained was—would it work?

"All right," said Sparky. "It's time to save Frankie."

Carefully, the ghouls lifted their friend into the Recharge Chamber. Ghoulia swapped Frankie's bolts and set them right. Sparky connected two cables from the Recharger to the bolts. Everything was in place.

Sparky made a few final adjustments, and a single spark discharged from the lens and hit the control panel of the time portal. It hummed. It was on! The lens was beginning to spin. The blue vortex was appearing…and a shadowy figure was emerging…

But nobody noticed any of this. They were

concentrating on the Recharge Chamber—and Frankie.

"This has to work," whispered Draculaura.

"Let's create *life*!" exclaimed Sparky, throwing the switch. Electricity flowed from the Recharge Chamber into Frankie's bolts. Every part of her was glowing.

"C'mon, Frankie," said Clawdeen. "Come back to us."

Sparky increased the electricity. Frankie glowed a little brighter, but nothing else happened. She wasn't coming back to life. It wasn't working. Defeated, Sparky shut down the machine.

No one knew what to say.

"Maybe you're still missing something," said an authoritative voice.

Everyone whirled around. Standing in front of the time portal was Hexiciah Steam!

Sparky gulped nervously. "Professor?"

"Dad!" exclaimed Robecca, running over to hug him. "Oh, Dad, I missed you!"

The professor hugged her back and then held her at arm's length to get a good look at her. "Nice to meet you, my daughter. You're just perfect. It looks as though I did an amazing job on you. Or rather…I will do an amazing job…at some point."

Robecca hugged him again happily. Her dad was the best.

Hexiciah raised his mechanical hand and pointed at Sparky. "And you, Victor Frankenstein, are late for our conversation after class. By about two hundred years, if I'm not mistaken. I'm here to bring you back to our time, where you belong. But first it looks like we have a ghoul to save."

The professor began examining the Recharge Chamber. Sparky nervously explained everything. "I don't understand, Professor. I was sure *this* would work."

Professor Steam shook his head. "Didn't you listen to anything I said before? Creating life takes more than just what's up here."

"I know." Sparky sighed. "It takes the spark. But it's all gone. Frankie used it all up."

Hexiciah smiled indulgently. Sparky could be so smart—and still miss the most important things. "How can something be gone that's inside of *every* living thing?"

Sparky considered this, but it was Draculaura who understood it first. She shut her eyes and began rubbing her hands together, back and forth, until a little spark shot out.

"How'd you do that?" asked Clawdeen.

"I don't know! I just closed my eyes and thought about Frankie."

"So, we all have the spark?" asked Cleo.

"C'mon, everybody!" exclaimed Lagoona. "Think, together, of your best memory of Frankie."

All the ghouls and Fusions gathered around the Recharge Chamber, their eyes shut, concentrating.

"I remember when Frankie helped bring *me* back to life," said Robecca. Sparks flew from her fingers.

"She planned a surprise party for my sweet 1,600," remembered Draculaura, creating even more electricity.

Avia Trotter stepped forward. "She made us feel like we belong." All of the Fusions lit up at the thought of what Frankie had done for them.

Ghoulia was texting something on her iCoffin. She pressed send. All over Monster High, students' phones started binging with the message. Everyone began summoning up happy memories of Frankie. And it was so easy to do—she was one of the sweetest, friendliest monsters at Monster High.

"She freed me from the lantern," said Gigi the genie.

"She kept me from doing that dumb thing!" said Gil.

"She helped me find my lost love! Please! Save Frankie," pleaded Rochelle the gargoyle.

Sparky closed his eyes and concentrated.

Everyone and everything in the workshop was beginning to glow—not just with electricity but with love. A powerful current was flowing into Frankie. Suddenly, there was a brilliant flash of light that filled the entire room. It touched each and every one of their hearts.

When they opened their eyes, it had faded. Had anything happened to Frankie? Had she felt it?

"Did it work?" whispered Venus.

"Frankie?" called Cleo.

Bonita was chewing her sleeve nervously.

"Come back to us, Frankie," Robecca begged.

Clawdeen sighed. "Ghoulfriend, if you're taking your sweet time for dramatic effect, you're killin' us over here."

They waited. Nothing was happening. Hope seemed to be lost.

But then, Frankie sat up, just like that, smiling. "Did I miss anything?"

"Frankie!"

"She's back!"

"It worked!"

The ghouls pounced on Frankie, all trying to hug her at once.

"I did it! I created life!" shouted Sparky. Everyone glared at him. "*We* did it," he corrected himself.

Hexiciah was opening the time portal again. "All right, Victor Frankenstein. It's time to go."

Sparky looked at Frankie for a long time. "Thank you," he said at last.

She smiled. "I told you it was possible to create life."

"No, not for that," said Sparky, shaking his head. "Thank you for showing me that I am not alone. That I *do* have a family."

Shyly, Sparky reached out to hug Frankie.

"Take care of yourself...Grandpa." Frankie laughed.

Sparky smirked and headed to the time vortex. Just before stepping into it, he reached down and grabbed a bolt from the floor. Frankie had a feeling he wasn't done with getting into trouble.

Robecca waved to her father. "Miss you already!"

He grinned and let out a steam whistle. The light in the vortex swirled and brightened. They were gone!

CHAPTER 22

IN THE SPOTLIGHT

The screen behind Frankie Stein was filled with light. Her story was over. She had told the whole school about her adventures with her grandpa Sparky. The entire auditorium had been hushed as she told them about how her friends had brought her back to life.

"Which brings us to the end of our bite-centennial celebration," she announced from the stage. "But our story doesn't end there…"

The curtain opened, the spotlight widened, and standing onstage with Frankie were all her ghoulfriends and the Fusions.

"The story of Monster High is being written every single day," Frankie continued. "And as we move forward into the future, we will continue our rich tradition of accepting anybody who walks through those doors, whether they're vampire or werewolf, creepy or freaky...or Fusion."

Frankie noticed that Bonita was chewing on her sleeve again. "It's okay," she said. "You're one of us now. Together we are Monster High!"

People in the audience began to clap wildly. Someone cheered. Everyone was on their feet giving Frankie a standing ovation.

"Bravo! Bravo! Bravo!" shouted Mr. Where.

Next to him, Abbey Bominable wrinkled her nose. "You stink like yak fur. This is intentional?"

Frankie held up her hands to silence everyone. "So that's our little story," she concluded. "The Fusions have found the home they were looking for. Sparky, er, Grandpa Victor went back to his own time, where he used the secret of the spark to build the family *he* was looking for...and even though my ghoulfriends aren't fused together anymore, they're still pretty much inseparable. Oh, and spending all that time as a Fusion really sparked Clawdeen's imagination."

On the screen flashed a shot from one of Clawdeen's sketchpads showing all kinds of new freaky Fusion fashions.

"How claw-some are those designs?" said Frankie, and the audience was on their feet applauding again. "And as for me? Let's just say that after a crazy family adventure like that, I had plenty of information for my scaritage project."

She snapped her fingers, and the screen showed her family album—now filled with photos.

"Check it out," said Frankie. "That's the *real* family photo album. Turns out my parents knew they couldn't tell me about Grandpa until after we'd met each other and discovered the secret of the spark. Otherwise things wouldn't have happened the way they were supposed to. Seriously, thinking about all this time-travel logic would make my head spin if it wasn't sewn on. But hey, this time I got an A on my project."

In the audience, Mr. Rotter flipped his pencil. It bounced off his head.

Frankie laughed. "Favorite student, right here!"

Frankie noticed that Neighthan was right beside her. She smiled shyly. "So does this mean you'll stick around for a while?"

He grabbed her hand and pulled her close. "I wouldn't miss being part of this freaky family!"

Frankie's bolts shot out sparks. Love was in the air!

CHAPTER 23

GHOUL-SCAPADES

Frankie Stein got an A on her scaritage report, Monster High got some voltageous new students, and Ghoulia got a brand-new laboratory. The very next day she moved her things into Hexiciah Steam's old workshop.

She updated it with modern equipment and laptops and cleaned out most of the cobwebs. Already, she had some experiments she wanted to try out. After a long time scribbling calculations and inputting numbers to her computer, she headed over to the control panel for the time-travel lens.

The lens began spinning, the glowing portal appeared, and just like that, Ghoulia stepped into it and disappeared.

Hours later, the workshop was still and quiet. All of a sudden, the lens began to spin, the vortex appeared, and Ghoulia jumped out. Her clothes were in tatters. She'd ripped off her shirtsleeve and tied it around her head like a headband. Dirt was smeared across her face like war paint. She was carrying a long wooden stick, and on the end of it was a stone arrowhead.

She whirled around.

The head of a giant T-Rex lunged through the portal and snapped at her.

Ghoulia whacked it with her stick and forced it back into the vortex. She slammed her stick onto the control panel and the portal closed.

She wiped her brow and laughed.

Groan! That was close!